W   Ell, Flynn J.
        Dakota scouts.

JUL 20 1992

$18.95

DATE			

D1292210

ELL, FLYNN J   06/19/92
DAKOTA SCOUTS
(3) 1992 F

DAKOTA SCOUTS

DAKOTA SCOUTS

Flynn J. Ell

Walker and Company
New York

For my mother, Isabelle

iJUL 2 0 1992

First published in the United States of America in 1992
by Walker Publishing Company, Inc.

Published simultaneously in Canada by Thomas Allen & Son
Canada, Limited, Markham, Ontario

Library of Congress Cataloging-in-Publication Data
Ell, Flynn J.
Dakota scouts / Flynn J. Ell.
p. cm.
ISBN 0-8027-4130-4
1. Dakota Indians—Wars—Fiction. I. Title
PS3555.L5166D3   1992
813′.54—dc20   91-45384
CIP

Printed in the United States of America

2 4 6 8 10 9 7 5 3 1

CHAPTER 1

LONE Bear flattened his bronze body in the cavity of an old eagle-trapping pit and peered down through the spears of a yucca. The spiny plant broke the outline of his head on the horizon. He watched a white soldier who had left his big horse tied to a handy clump of sage. The soldier scooped water past his dusty lips with his right hand while he steadied his crouched body with his left. His eyes squinted beneath his hatbrim. A canteen hung from his shoulder, and gumbo oozed up at the edge of his boot soles. The man's coming would be visible from his footprints to other users of the small spring until rain erased his sign. It was surprising to see that a white could discover the small water gift so far off the main trails.

The Sioux wanted the soldier's dark bay. The animal's hide glistened in the sun. Lone Bear's brothers in the Fox Society would envy him. Little Moon would be proud, although she would only say it with her dark eyes.

He wanted to humiliate the invader, too, by putting him afoot. The soldier must be a scout like he, for rarely did these enemies travel alone through the land of the Dacotah. Lone Bear schemed to mount his own fleet pony, swoop down the steep slope, grab the prize from his unwary foe, and be out of range of the trooper's pistol before the white man could react.

John Benson whirled from his bent position and set his boots squarely. At the same time his .44-caliber, army Colt seemed to jump from its holster into his wet hand. He fired. The lead slug kicked up a puff of dust at the butte's edge near the yucca.

"Try it, and you meet the Great Spirit in person," Benson said, scrambling to dry ground and his horse.

Fine clay sand sprayed Lone Bear's face before he rolled deeper into the trapping pit. He slithered along the short trench, raced back to his pony, and mounted. Like two made one, he and the pony fled down the winding trail on the butte's backside. The narrow path led into a deep gully. Lone Bear tugged gently on the braided rawhide rein fixed to the hackamore on his pony's jaw, slowing the pony to a rocking lope. He doubted the soldier dared follow him and run the risk of an ambush, even though the soldier carried guns.

Benson, too, mounted and spurred his big bay to a gallop away from the butte. They cut through openings in the silver sage. The soldier wasn't sure if the Indian was a loner or the lead man of a war party. His own objective was complete. General Stanley had sent him out to scout for Indians who might be flanking the column of troops five miles south. John Benson now knew at least one was, and the Indian had come in close on him in broad daylight. A man's thirst could cost him his life on the prairie even if water could be found. Benson had not even gotten to fill his canteen.

Lone Bear, retreating the opposite way, checked his pony. He slid from the pony's back and crawled quickly up the bank to peer across the flat. He saw a brown plume of dust rising above the soldier and his running horse. He coveted that horse and the soldier's rifle, so foolishly left in its scabbard. If Lone Bear had had the gun, the prize bay would be his, and the soldier's woman would wail his death song.

He must return to Sitting Bull's Hunkpapa camp—they would be pleased to learn the horse soldiers were still careless. The Indian mounted his pony, and they crawled through the deep gully for another mile before they trotted into the open. A jackrabbit exploded out of a clump of bunchgrass, and the horse shied. Lone Bear's legs clenched the pony's ribs, and it calmed. The horse threw its head frantically, its ears stiffening.

Lone Bear heard the snake, too. His horse's back arched, trying to unload its heavy burden and flee from the sound. Lone Bear, rein in hand, jumped to the ground and put himself between the high-pitched whirr and his mount. He spotted the snake before it struck from a coiled position.

"Ah, brother snake, we're too big a meal for you today," the Indian said calmly. The snake's rattling tail slowed, its tongue darting in and out to taste that truth.

Lone Bear led his calmed horse to a nearby granite boulder. The animal ate prairie grass while the rider took a handful of dried buffalo meat from a rawhide pouch on his bone saddle. The sun beat on them. Horseflies attacked their legs. They must find good water and a safe place to rest before striking out for the Hunkpapa camp. It was a good day's ride.

Benson slowed his bay and scanned the flat country around him. A herd of thirty-five pronghorns stood eyeing him from about three hundred yards. Still edgy, he was relieved that he wasn't pursued. He guessed he would cut ahead of the trail of the troop column if he continued south. His eyes searched for dust rising off the prairie.

A ridge of foam had formed on the bay's neck after the run. His horse, however, had plenty of reserve energy.

In close, that Indian would have outmaneuvered him, but the cavalry mount was hard to beat for power. It was chance alone that sent the magpie flying away from the butte and brought his attention to the yucca. Benson allowed that if the Indian had ducked his camouflaged head two inches lower, the outcome from their encounter might have been different. He counted himself lucky. He hadn't suspected another human soul would be stirring within ten miles. Benson figured the Indian wanted his horse, or he would have come charging earlier on his pony. And he must have been Sioux. Even the friendly Crow might try to steal a man's horse, but not alone in this mean land of their enemies. The Sioux must have been watching him for some time before their meeting, or he wouldn't have got in so close.

Benson found the column gliding snakelike along the course of the Heart River. He remained out of rifle range—no sense risking some nervous trooper getting excited by his approach and taking potshots at him. Some greenhorns never learned to tell the difference between a buffalo and a horse at a distance, let alone a white man and a red man. He finally loped his bay at an easy pace toward the column's head.

He neared the battalion's fluttering guidon, and he heard the muffled ripple of men shouting, "Scout coming in! Scout coming in!"

Benson saw a rider break off from the lead troopers and ride toward him. "The general's anxious to hear your report," Sergeant Sean Collins said, drawing his horse up beside Benson's bay.

"Not much," said Benson, continuing to let his horse lope and veer toward the column.

"Let's have it, Private. Any of them redskins out there or not?"

"Sioux, Sergeant."

"Sioux! How many?"

Benson was silent for a while before answering.

"One. Just one. Five miles out. Maybe a scout. Missed him with a shot. He hightailed it, heading north."

"Oh boy. Wait till the general hears. His buns will burn. Those railroad surveyors will brown their trousers. No flickering fires, just cold chow. Good job, Benson."

Collins broke away and rode toward the head of the column at a pace that laid his horse's ears back flat and dropped the animal's belly six inches closer to the ground. Chunks of clay erupted under its shod hooves, spiraled upward ten feet, and arched back to earth.

Benson watched. One lone Indian sighting, and the whole column would probably go crazy. He wouldn't be surprised if some of the greenhorns started shooting at sagebrush. Benson wondered if the Indians were as jumpy. Probably not. Collins would be back to get full details of the encounter for a final report when Major General David Stanley had his castle built for the evening. After reports of the ruggedness of the Badlands ahead, the drunken commander finally decided to send his army band back home.

Benson had signed on with the Seventh Cavalry at Fort Abraham Lincoln. Rode into Bismarck one day from Illinois where there were just too many good people. *Go West, young man;* he read the 1873 railroad ads in newspapers, and they made Dakota Territory sound like a golden paradise. Fertile land? It turned out to be just grass. Oceans of grass. This could be good cattle country, and Benson figured he might take a chunk of the land for his own ranch when the railroad was in and the hostiles were subdued.

Benson dismounted when he got to the troops. He slipped the bit from his bay's mouth and hooked the halter rope to the pack of a mule waddling along in the fog of dust engulfing the troopers. He grabbed a chunk of hardtack and greasy piece of cooked bacon from his saddlebag and walked beside the black man who was leading the string of mules.

"Howdy, John Benson," said Isaiah Dorman. "Your coming in stirred up the men. See anything?"

"One Sioux. Jumped me at a spring five miles out. Do you think he was with Sitting Bull?"

"Why do you white people say 'Sitting Bull' all the time? You know there's a lot more Indians out there than just old Sitting Bull."

Dorman had lived with the Sioux and spoke their language. He knew more about what was in all that sagebrush than Benson did after just riding through it. He also knew the big chief personally. Occasionally called him by his native handle, "Tantanka Iyotake." He said the Sioux leader saw something spiritual about Dorman's own blackness. The Indians called him "Teat," after the dark color of a buffalo cow's udder, the nourishing place from which flowed the blessings of the great Pte to the people.

"The Sioux like to keep an eye on the white men," said Dorman, softly. His dark eyes swept the horizon from one side of the column to the other. "The general better put out more scouts quick if he wants to know if the Sioux are coming before they get here. They sure like them fine horses and shiny guns the troopers have."

Benson bit down hard on the biscuit. It almost knocked out a tooth.

"I got some cheese stowed under that pack," Dorman said, nodding his head toward a canvas-covered lump on the lead mule. "Fresh water, too."

"You've got a bit of angel under that hard hide of yours," said Benson, pulling out the small roll of stiff cloth.

The water gurgled and tasted cool from being wrapped and kept in the shade.

"How'd you find water like this?" Benson asked.

"I can smell it, John Benson, just like one of them Indians. They taught me that."

"Why did you leave them?"

"A man like me needs money, same as a man like you. I just left. We still get along."

Dorman had a Santee Sioux woman at Fort Rice who claimed he was her slave. Dorman said it was their private joke, but he never did say if he had ever really been a slave to anyone. He could ride, scout, and speak Sioux, and he could handle a string of mules as gently as a good schoolmarm could tend children. He took a liking to Benson when he noticed the scout also was a loner in the long line of blue troopers. Dorman was cozier with the Sioux than the army cared to see, but they liked his credentials otherwise. The black man didn't say much about how he came to live with the Santee Sioux who were blamed for the Minnesota massacre. Benson didn't like to pry, but figured the woman probably had a hand in it. He'd known a few women back East who almost sucked him into their families, too. But they would never have put up with letting him ride West and join the cavalry the way Dorman's woman did.

Lone Bear found a shallow cave carved under a sandstone outcrop that looked like a good spot to rest. It was halfway up one hill in a medium-sized string of rolling hills overlooking the expanse of grass and sage below. The hill was laced with game trails, and its gully was buried under chokecherry and juniper bushes. The Indian fashioned a hobble from the rein of his hackamore and turned his pony loose in the brush to graze. A small trickle of water leaked from a fissure in the outcrop, and he captured some in cupped hands and drank. He took his only blunt-pointed arrow from his quiver and walked to a point where the grass and undergrowth met in an accommodating union.

He hungered for fresh meat of any kind, even though he could make no fire. If he got none, he would eat more of the dried venison he carried. It was too early in the year for berries, but camas plants were in bloom and he would eat their roots flavored with wild onions. The white man carried his supplies in heavy wagons. The Indian knew Mother Earth was filled with a harvest she pushed forward regularly from her bosom. He thanked Grandfather and all of his helpers for the bounty of plants and brother animals.

He missed a shot at a cottontail rabbit that skipped past within a rock's throw of where he crouched. He retrieved his arrow. If he had more time, he would make a snare from a strand of muscle tissue taken from his last buffalo kill that he had tucked in his rawhide parfleche. The sun was lowering itself to end the day. A red glow filled the evening sky, but Thunderbeings were lighting their torches in scattered spots along the horizon. Lone Bear lay down on a matte of grass he had gathered. He would sleep without fire and rise when the sun renewed him and the sagging yellow and purple flowers of late spring.

Brother coyote and brother owl made their evening calls. Their sounds reassured Lone Bear that only those with night vision were moving about.

Benson made his full report to Collins and was told to be ready at first light to renew scouting. Reports of other scouts had come in empty, but rumors built of an impending attack by Sioux, as word spread that Benson had been jumped *"by a war party of forty braves."* The scout was helpless to stop the rumor officers encouraged to keep the men alert.

Lightning flashes illuminated roiling dark clouds. It looked like a squall might hit the camp. Collins had been right. No fires. As if the Indians didn't already know where the soldiers were.

"Looks like bad weather's coming, John Benson," Dorman told him when he came to turn his mount out to graze. "I got a big tarp I'm willing to share with you. Unless you got other plans."

Benson enjoyed the black man's company. He knew this country. It was Dorman who told him to watch the birds and animals if he wanted to read the terrain. Said, "John Benson, those maps officers spread on tables just talk a little bit. When you see a coyote looking back instead of at you, you best find out quick what he's looking at. And anytime you see birds flying away and they ain't flying away from you—they're flying from something you ought to know about."

Dorman told him the birds and animals are talking all the time and that a man will keep his hair a lot longer if he listens to what they have to say.

"I'll take you up on that offer," said Benson. "It looks like we may get doused before this night's over. Couldn't have kept any fires lit even if General Booze Breath allowed them."

"John Benson, don't let the general hear you calling him 'Booze Breath.' The general don't take kindly to jokes about his drinking." He paused. "I know what you mean, though. He likes to take his nips."

Scattered raindrops popped open heavily on the tarp in the darkness to signal the arrival of clouds Benson had seen coming. Thunder banged its deep voice into the ground around them. The prairie visible through the entrance of the makeshift tent turned bright daylight briefly when lightning struck nearby. Then blackness jumped back over it. Benson could still see stars blinking clearly in the deepness of space. It was as if God were picking on them. Rain fell in torrents amid what seemed a natural cannon bombardment. The tarp began to flap wildly, and hailstones ripped a wide slice down Dorman's side. Cold air rushed through the opening. Both men were sitting up and reaching for their boots when the wet mass of canvas collapsed on them.

By the time they clawed their way to the edges of the heavy cloth, the thick sheet of rain and hail was moving away and only a vapor of light drops continued to fall. Horses and mules grunted. Officers shouted at the men to hold it down. They cursed and slipped in the dark.

"I found it, John Benson," Dorman said. "That rope

peg pulled right out of the ground. I can get it back up if you help pull the rope."

"God, I'll bet it's drier than a bone a hundred yards from here," Benson said.

"We got trouble enough, John Benson, without you complaining. Maybe God is trying to tell us something."

"He is just reminding us that we've got problems out here, with or without the Sioux."

Benson could hear Dorman scuffling in the dark. The scout himself stripped nude and tossed his longjohns on the renewed tarp top. He crawled back to bed to shiver the remaining hours of night away until dawn. He might have been in a cozy ranch home made of railroad ties covered by a tight sod roof. He'd seen the homes of settlers along the tracks being laid from the East. This country could use some civilizing, but not too much. Those sodbusters were just about as sorry a bunch as the Indians. He hoped that Sioux out there enjoyed the storm, too.

Lone Bear rose with the sun, circled the hill he had slept on, and noted no other humans were in sight. He stripped leaves from a sage plant and moved to the sunward side of his camp. He rubbed the leaves between his fingers, and as the pungent odor rose from his hands, he spread them wide at arm's length and began a muffled chant.

> Oh, Grandfather, who made all things,
> I call on you.
> Lead me to the camp of my people safely,
> I call on you.
> Help to keep me hidden from my enemies,
> I call on you.
> Oh, Grandfather, thank you for all things,
> I call on you.

Lone Bear fetched his horse from the brushy draw and snapped a few juniper berries from a tree he passed. He chewed them to freshen his mouth.

"Iktomi, we must find our people and warn that it is true horse soldiers are riding in our land again," he said softly to his pony. It can come to no good. The whites seem to be showing up everywhere. None of the big trails are safe anymore. Who had sent these white, mean animals to destroy the Indians?

He longed to gaze on Little Moon. Constantly changing camps and moving was hard on both women and old people. The wind was picking up, and Lone Bear turned his pony's nose into it, for he knew that Sitting Bull and the other chiefs had made their camp to the north of his position. The whites were not yet traversing the Place Where They Kill the Deer as heavily as new trails showing their wagon tracks along the Heart River. What plans could the chiefs make? It was going bad for all Indians. But some were getting guns from traders.

Lone Bear knew his life would flower if he had a gun. He had seen a warrior drop a bull buffalo in its tracks from twice the range of his bow. It was the lack of guns that kept the Sioux fighters from overrunning these white enemies. Maybe with guns the red men would drive the whites out, or at least come to terms with them.

He hungered again for that soldier's horse and gun. Maybe the white chiefs would send more of their scouts out to check on Indians. Maybe Grandfather would smile on him if he tried again. The march of the horse soldiers was not in the direction of Sitting Bull's camp. What if the chiefs doubted his word because he brought back no proof of his skirmish with the white man?

Lone Bear pressed his right knee into Iktomi's side and eased back on his left leg, and the animal veered obediently to the new direction, southward.

CHAPTER 2

LONE Bear watched the soldiers break camp in the haziness of fog rising from the heating prairie. Horses and mules were gathered from their pickets in the rear and brought forward. Bridles and harness jingled. The Indian hooked his legs firmly to the back and midriff of Iktomi and hung close to the animal's neck, which he bit sharply where the flabby ridge joined the mane. Lone Bear steeled his mind to the reaction to his daring that was sure to come from the white men. The pony exploded into a full gallop aimed at the straggling tail of the horse herd. They bore down on the fleet gray mare that had escaped from two herders and was loping away from the column through the sage. The horse trailed a lead rope. It was a fine mare that held its head up and bowed to the side.

The Indian's left arm was touching the lead rope attached to the mare's halter before the first puff of dirt flew up in front of Iktomi's charge. The sound of the shot came next, then more puffs of dirt and a chorus of shouts as Lone Bear sat erect on his horse's back, caught the rope, and raced away with the already loping mare picking up to full speed behind him. He had surprised the white soldiers. He would make it to the edge of the Badlands a short distance ahead and hide with the mare in its deep gorges before they got mounted.

The lead rope nearly jerked Lone Bear from Iktomi's back. Behind him the gray mare crumpled to its knees and blood spurted from a gaping hole in its chest. The animal's nostrils flared, and its eyes widened in fear. It sank in the dust and quivered as Lone Bear released the rope. He bent low behind his pony, as bullets whined overhead and kicked up puffs of dirt all around him. Lone Bear's face was wet, and he feared he was hit. The soldiers would come. They would find him toppled from his horse.

He could feel the stiffness of Iktomi's hooves slamming into the ground. Lone Bear wiped his free hand across his face as he and the horse slid from the flat prairie down into the edge of the Badlands. Jutting pink and gray buttes sprouted junipers which shielded him. The fluid he wiped was clear and frothy, not blood red. It was only saliva whipped back by the wind from his horse's mouth.

The white men would have to work harder to take his spirit today. His medicine worked. A small rawhide bundle hiding an eagle's beak dangled from his neck and flailed his bare chest. He sorrowed for the mare that had been brought down by its masters' bullets in such a cowardly way. The white men hold nothing sacred.

Benson himself was somewhere between eating hardtack and corned beef in a can, cursing the general for not allowing fire for coffee, and getting his still-wet gear together when he heard Dorman.

"You're asking for a heap of trouble," the black man said, firmly, his eyes directed toward the rear of the column.

The remark's hardness coaxed Benson to look up in time to see the charge of the lone Sioux.

"He's after our horses," Benson said, his voice tinged with disbelief when he got his eyes focused on the intruder.

A shot rang out, kicking up dust near the Indian and his pony.

"All hell's about to break loose," Dorman said, heading to his pack for his six-gun.

An officer shouted for the bugler to sound the alarm.

Men nearby scrambled for their carbines; scattered shoot-ing had already begun. Where that Indian came from was anybody's guess, but it was apparent he was heading for the breaks. Dorman said a Sioux and his horse could melt into the plains effortlessly the way a prairie chicken's pinnated black, gray, and white feathers made it invisible to the human eye when the bird was right underfoot.

Benson saw an officer run out of his tent with a Sharps rifle. His hot voice shouted orders at Sergeant Collins, who cursed two men trying to saddle a spirited, light-gray gelding.

"Here it comes," Benson said.

The distance was at least five hundred yards to the Sioux and facing into the sun seeping through the haze and grayness of dawn. The officer pressed the rifle against the corner of his wall tent. The Sharps bellowed deeply over the dull thump of Springfield carbines sporadically answering the single Indian's charge. Some of the soldiers shot into clumps of sage, anything big enough to hide a man. Benson saw the officer squeeze off the round that brought down the horse behind the Sioux. The officer slapped his thigh in approval.

"Get your horse," Collins yelled at Benson as the ser-geant ran past toward the small picket line that roped off the mounts of scouts and junior aides to the general. Benson was scrambling to comply when the officer on the gray and three other mounted men galloped by, nearly trampling him and Dorman.

Benson's boot hit the metal stirrup hanging from the flat military saddle astride his bay at the same time Collins went charging after the officers. But instead of following, the scout cut straight across from the column and entered the Badlands a quarter mile west of the Indian. His hunch was the nervy red man would circle back north, and there was a fifty-fifty chance he'd come his way. Chasing the Indian direct might be good sport for officers, but it was dangerous because of the possibility of ambushes. Besides, Dorman had cautioned him against riding with a crowd. The old man had said just look at a pile of manure. "See how all that horse dung brings on flies. Don't bunch up like that, and the flies won't land all over you." Benson disdained running with the pack anyway.

The uproar of the camp behind him faded as Benson's horse slid onto a game trail that wobbled down a hillside and led to a flat stretch of creek bottom, broken by jutting buttes. The whole column could hide within a quarter of a mile, and it would take a month for anyone to find them.

That Indian was crafty. How many other Indians might be out there right now? Was this the same horse thief who had jumped him at the spring? What did that idiot have in mind? Buy a horse and save your red hide. Or steal one from some settlers.

Sneaking up on a lone soldier was calculated insanity, but attacking an entire column of soldiers led by a general—it was almost admirable, in the way one could admire a rattler's efficient killing fangs. Admirable, but dangerous.

Benson slowed his bay and gave the animal its head while he tried to get his mind to think Indian, but it was useless. He couldn't think like a rattlesnake either. His horse shied at a covey of sharptail grouse erupting from a clump of grass at the edge of a small pool of stagnant water.

"Settle down," he said firmly. The bay's black ears twitched back at the sound of his voice and steadied. Benson held to the winding edge of junipers and brush that met the grass in the creek bottom. It afforded some cover and gave him a chance to watch the flat and everything opposite his position. He also eyed the trail in front of him and swept the high spots. He moved forward slowly. He figured the officers and Collins would spook the Indian deeper into the Badlands.

He still couldn't believe the audacity. If those Indians could get together a surprise attack at dawn like that, they'd run the army plumb out of the country. That Indian was some rider. Benson had at first thought the charging Sioux's horse was riderless. Only Dorman's keen sight and the animal's speed had opened his own eyes to what was really happening.

Lone Bear had punished Iktomi long enough with hard running. He was riding the flats and veering through low passageways separating the buttes. If this was to be a test of endurance, let the white men know that he would not be easy to get. When Iktomi strained at a climb, Lone Bear slipped from his pony's back and ran behind the animal, holding Iktomi's tail. The white men had to guess where he was, or take time to follow what trail he left. If they got close, he would hear them first. Their horses jingled with noise from the metal bits in their mouths. His mount left only spongy dents in the padded undergrowth.

Lone Bear was proud of his daring. He had counted coup on the soldiers. The chiefs would call for a song to be made for him once the details of his feat reached their ears. Maybe his deed would be confirmed by the exchanges the white man's Indians carried on with his people in their secret trading sessions on the prairie. Even though Grandfather had chosen to keep him from taking a new horse home today, Little Moon would admire his bravery and know he was capable of keeping their tipi supplied with meat from brother buffalo. Enough so that her uncles wouldn't have to share their kills with her manless mother and young brother, Poke, who was not ready yet to go on a hunting party.

Lone Bear's thoughts distracted him. The shallow little river slithered ahead in the distance. He would cross, strike off farther into the Badlands, and cut back north to Sitting Bull's camp. The crusty layer of gumbo Iktomi trotted over buckled, and the horse plunged. Lone Bear instinctively pulled hard on the pony's hackamore to lay him on his side. The dull pop of a bone breaking reached Lone Bear's ears even as he pushed away from his horse's back to avoid its rolling body.

A gloomy mist poured into his mind. Lone Bear came to his feet with the rein in hand and tugged gently to bring Iktomi to a standing position. The pony struggled and squealed in pain. Only three legs moved. The left front hung limply in the crack of dry clay, which had invisibly housed a drainage from the butte to the river bottom. He had no choice. His knife blade pierced deeply into the lower side of the animal's neck near the jaw. Blood streamed from the wound, and silently the horse's struggle wound down. Lone Bear could hear the voices of men shouting to one another on his backtrail. He ran to the thick brush skirting the river and fell to his hands and knees to crawl into an opening. Thorns speared his bare flesh as he drew deeper into the maze of darkness. He moved toward the sound of the river swirling around a bend and crouched silently to listen.

The first shots he heard were met by a muffled echo. The white mens' voices sounded harsh. They must be shooting at the still form of Iktomi. They loved to kill so strongly that even the dead weren't sacred. And then the searing path of lead slamming through the brittle twigs of brush filled his ears. Lone Bear dove silently into a pool of water formed by the swirling river and swam under the surface to the base of a beaver lodge he saw protruding from the surface. He felt its ridges in the darkness and slipped beneath. Arms and hands clawing at the underside, he ripped through the lodge opening to push his head through the enlarged hole. The musty air fed his bursting lungs, and enough light entered from the lodge top to ensure it was unoccupied. The Indian hung there listening as shots thumped the undergrowth on the bank above. The length of the strafing seemed endless to the shivering Sioux. More loud, harsh voices sounded. And finally quiet. Lone Bear's body was numb with cold, and he couldn't stop his teeth from chattering. He had managed to wedge his body to the waist into the old beaver lodge and was thankful even in his fear. He couldn't tell how long he hung there.

Benson, too, had struck the Little Missouri River, and the first shots fired were carried along the channel to his ears. He changed his plan and headed upstream in the southerly direction from which the crazy little river flowed. How could that bunch of yahoo officers have caught up with the fleeing Indian? What were they shooting at? The small mixture of firing did not signal a pitched battle.

It was Collins who rode back to him when he came into view of the officers returning to camp.

"We got him. We killed his horse and got him," Collins panted when he trotted his mount up to Benson.

"Where is he?"

"He crawled into that brush and died. The captain said it was too much of trouble to search for the body. You check it out. We're heading back to make sure there're no more lunatics on the loose." Collins whirled his horse and charged off after the officers disappearing over a ridge.

Benson rode up on the Indian pony, dismounted, and shook his head. The bullet-riddled carcass also bore the telltale sign that its throat had been cut, and its left front leg still hung limply into the crack it made in the earth. The story of the animal's death was as plain for him to read as the page of a book. Benson mounted and rode down to the edge of the brush. He slid from the saddle, tied his bay to a branch, and drew his revolver. Cautiously, he worked his way along the edge of the brush, peering into its dark recesses and checking the sand for a show of where the Indian entered. He came to the indentations he was looking for and dropped to his knees to get a better view of the body he expected to see, but only a dark hole peered back at him. Benson bent deeper and crawled forward into the thicket.

"That dead Indian sure didn't lose much blood before he died," he mumbled to himself. Instinct took over, and he scrambled to turn around and retreat to the bright light entering the thicket behind him. His gray undershirt tangled in a thornbush. He thrashed around to free himself and get back into the open. Benson's ears heard the muffled clatter of horse hooves as he broke free in time to see his bay gallop away from him toward a crossing on the river. The Colt vibrated in his hand as he squeezed off six successive rounds at the fleeing Indian who seemed shielded by a magical cloak.

"You stinking, no good, thieving redskin snake," Benson shouted at the Indian, who raced across the river on his bay sending spray high behind them. The Sioux guided the animal to a narrow gap in the buttes which toppled raggedly to meet the river bottom. His horse and the Indian faded from Benson's view.

Benson glowered. How did the Sioux survive the hail of lead chucked at him this morning? The Indian had really worked his tail off for his prize, but Benson longed to pay the Indian back some day.

Shouting children ran beside Lone Bear as he entered the camp astride the bay cavalry mount. He pulled the lever-action Winchester from its scabbard, swung his right leg up over the horse's neck, and leapt cleanly from its back. Leading the animal, Lone Bear walked to meet several braves who had descended from cliffs where they were positioned as lookouts above a circle of tipis.

Deer carcasses hung from poles, and women were busy scraping hides. His eyes searched for the form of Little Moon, but he did not see her. The first to approach him was his uncle, Black Weasel.

"I see you have a new horse," Black Weasel said. "We were not sure until you drew closer if some ignorant white man was riding to our camp. But an Indian doesn't bounce like a jackrabbit when his horse trots." His eyes drifted admiringly to the rifle that hung in Lone Bear's narrow hand. "Come, you must be hungry and have much to tell us. You have been gone five days. A long time to scout on dry food. Have you been wrestling with a mountain cat?"

The men walked toward a tipi where Black Weasel's feathered lance stood outside its opening, signaling he was in residence at the camp. His woman, Takes Her Time, dipped broth into gourds from a skin pot hanging from poles. The pot sagged from the weight of hot stones it held. She handed soup and chunks of meat to the men as they passed into the dwelling and formed a circle around Black Weasel.

Lone Bear drank deeply of the warm broth and felt the strength of his body renew itself. He had ridden two days, circling deep into the Badlands before heading north to follow the winding stream past the camp in the Place Where They Kill the Deer. Then he cut south to the camp. He passed the rifle to the circle of men, each of whom fondled it gently before giving it to the next warrior seated beside him. Lone Bear's eyes barely contained his pride. Few of his brothers in the Fox Society had guns. No one had a repeating rifle. They worked the Winchester's lever action and sighted along its octagonal barrel. When they had eaten, Black Weasel lit his long-stemmed pipe, drew deeply, and passed it to Lone Bear seated at his left. No one spoke until the pipe completed a circle and returned to Black Weasel.

"We can see you have met the white man, Lone Bear, but we cannot tell how many there are. You must tell all things. Leave nothing out. Sitting Bull has told the council of his bad dreams. Grandfather has turned his face from the red man."

Lone Bear spoke to the circle of faces of his first meeting at the spring with the white man who rode the bay. Of how the clever soldier had fired at him. Of his sorrow at failing to get the horse. Of his determination to try again. Of the large size of the military column crossing Sioux land. Of his charge and escape into the Badlands, and finally how Grandfather had smiled on him and given him both the bay horse and lever rifle. The men grunted "hoka hey" as the details were related. The meeting broke off, and his uncle told Lone Bear that the council would hear of his feats that night.

Lone Bear went to search for a medicine man to doctor the wounds scratched in his torso and bare legs by the thicket of thorns. His body was wracked with pain, but he allowed no outward sign of it to reach the eyes of any who watched him stride through the camp. His happiness would be complete if he slept tonight by the side of Little Moon, if she dared come to him. The old ones were less stringent about marital ceremony now while their cares turned to survival and trying to stay clear of the deep trails white people made with their wagons through Sioux hunting grounds. Council meetings were being torn apart with debate on whether more attacks should be made against the whites, or if Indians should parley with them. It seemed that no white man's word was good. Each new attempt at treaty was littered with lies and distortions since the whites had found the worthless yellow metal in the Shining Mountains. Now they came like hornets that could not be turned back.

By the time Lone Bear had bathed under a tiny waterfall tumbling over a rock, the quarter moon was peering brightly from a twinkling dark blue sky. An old man had mixed a paste from herbs and dabbed his wounds while chanting to his spirit helpers and rattling a gourd filled with seeds. Lone Bear's bed of boughs had been fashioned in a thicket at the edge of the camp, and he lay down with his arms behind his head. He could see the stars overhead through an opening above him. A rustling in the brush startled him, and he grasped the handle of his knife.

"Lone Bear," he heard a woman's voice whisper. "Lone Bear, be not afraid. It is only I."

The young scout released his grip on the knife, and he tried to calm his heart which thumped heavily against his chest. Blood rushed hotly through his body when a woman's hand brushed lightly over his legs as she lay next to him. Little Moon had never before come to him—perhaps she wished to celebrate his successful scout. In the darkness, he embraced her, expecting the slender body of Little Moon. But it was Braids Maker, who had no husband because she was unable to be true to one man. Lone Bear's passion was overshadowed by his disappointment. "Go," he said, pushing her back toward the entrance.

She slipped away from him and whispered, "Tell no one." As quietly as she had entered, Braids Maker left his lodge. Just before tiredness overcame him, he thought again of Little Moon, garbed in white buckskin, smiling to him, and then her image faded away in the deepness of his sleep.

CHAPTER 3

JOHN Benson poured a cup of coffee from the tin pot Isaiah Dorman had hanging on a tripod of willow sticks beside his wagon.

The general had given the all clear for day fires.

"Sure is a funny way to run an army," Dorman said. "With a war party jumping one of our best scouts and his escaping after they stole his horse, a man would think we'd be sleeping with one eye open and be ready all the time for more trouble."

"There was only that one Indian out there," said Benson.

"That ain't what the captain says—and Sergeant Collins is backing him. According to them, those officers killed that Sioux, and you got bushwhacked by the war party they run off. You sure are one lucky white man, John Benson."

"Rub it in, Isaiah."

The black man smiled as he poked the coals under the fire.

Benson drew a new mount from the horse herd and obtained a single-shot Springfield from the supply pack. It was one sorry piece of iron for a scout.

He did not care what kind of report Collins wished to make about the incident. But he knew there were a lot of buffalo chips dropping from the sergeant's pen. Rumor was the general regaled the other officers at their private supper table with stories of how to hit the Indians hard and fast and watch them run.

Collins ordered Benson to saddle up and ride the column's right flank. "Go deeper, Benson, and keep your eyes open. Now, you know how tricky those redskins are."

The scout rode out of camp on another bay, which, because of military conformation requirements, was almost a twin of the horse the Indian had stolen. Only this one had a big, humped nose. Benson decided he would call the horse Roman Nose.

It was a bright May day. Benson pulled up on a hill and watched the column mount and move out. The head of the long line of blue seemed to detach itself momentarily before the middle section lurched forward. Then, the bulge of pack mules ambled into action, and the long procession was moving behind its fluttering guidon. Benson shivered at the thought of the column's concentrated power and organization—all to protect a party of railroad surveyors and fight any Indians who got in the road.

"C'mon, Roman Nose, we've got to earn our pay." The cavalry mount shook its head and obediently turned toward open country. The line of troopers faded behind them, and Benson revived his senses. He hoped Dorman could come up with another repeating rifle for him. The only way Benson could get one for himself was if he brought in a fresh Indian scalp. The offer had been made by one of the general's junior officers—a rifle in exchange for a scalp.

Officers had the quick-shot weapons, and extras were carried in another of the special mule packs that General Stanley had loaded to meet their needs. According to the class system, those below officer level were vermin; above, gods to be envied. The general was at the top of the heap, with all coming into his presence bowing and scraping.

Benson and Dorman shared an unspoken dislike for the class system. To watch men with good educations yessing their so-called betters from sunup to sundown was disgusting. The scout was glad he didn't have to ride with the pack—or pack for their rides, as Dorman did.

A golden eagle soared and circled to the north. Benson watched the bird draw its wings together and plummet to the skyline before disappearing behind a ridge. The scout worked his way into a draw that led to the top. His horse broke into a trot, and Benson pulled Roman Nose in when they reached the high side. Three coyotes were running an antelope calf that had been spooked out of its hiding place by the sharp-eyed eagle. The mother ran helplessly in circles, diving toward the predators with its head bowed, then retreating. The eagle rose above the melee and floated on an updraft. The coyotes were oblivious to the approaching horse and rider, and the calf darted frantically, trying to elude them.

Benson cocked the single-shot, 45.70 Springfield and fired at the lead coyote. The animal rolled in a cloud of dust, came up yelping on three legs, and led the other two runners toward a grassy draw which quickly engulfed them. The calf circled to its mother, and they raced off together toward a bunch of their fellow critters, which had stood eyeing the contest, overcome by both their fear and curiosity.

"There, little fella. This was your lucky day," Benson said. He reloaded and brought Roman Nose back to the brush that skirted the ridge of hills he had crossed. He worried that the shot tipped off his location to Indians who might be trailing the column, but he always found himself siding with the underdog. He had been orphaned as a child and was acutely aware that young ones without protection are easy prey. Benson decided to head back east, circle north, and meet the column to the west somewhere in the Badlands.

He found himself crossing the gorge that had concealed the retreat of the Indian who had tried to steal his horse at the spring. The Indian pony's tracks stood out clear from those of deer that also used the trail as a route from their bedding grounds to the grassland. Benson couldn't resist, and he followed the Indian's path to the spot he had stopped his pony and left his own soft marks indented in the sand beside the game trail. Benson rode higher up the butte, dismounted, and bending low ascended toward its top. He worked his way across its flat surface until he neared the yucca plant that had hidden the Indian he had fired at from the spring.

Beneath him, a pair of scrawny warriors were crouched at the water's edge. One sat back at the border of the sagebrush Benson had used for a hitching post. He kept lookout while the other brave drew water into a rawhide bag. Benson tensed and cursed his stupidity for almost being caught offguard again at the same damned watering hole. He guessed the two Indians were not Sioux. Their bony horses were heavily loaded with furs, and they quickly mounted and continued their journey in a southerly direction away from the movement of the military column that must now be somewhere southwest of his own position.

Benson rode down to the spring, dismounted with his rifle in hand, and strode toward the water's muddy edge. His own previous footprints had been erased by the tracks of animals. He dumped the stagnant water in his canteen and refilled it with the clear, cold fluid from the small pond. He stepped back on Roman Nose and headed north.

Lone Bear had gone back out to watch the column of horse soldiers. Only now he sat astride the strong bay horse and carried the lever gun. He learned he could make his new horse veer by touching a rein to the animal's neck. The jingle of the bridle had been silenced when he replaced it with a hackamore, to which Lone Bear had added another rawhide rein until the new animal learned to work with one. The stiff cavalry saddle with its strange opening in the middle was replaced by his bone saddle. His bare legs clung to the animal's sides, giving Lone Bear a sense of oneness with the horse.

Lone Bear took with him a handful of the shiny cartridges he had found in the cavalry saddlebag. Black Weasel had shown him how to open the rifle by pushing down on the lever. He could then slip a shell into the barrel's dark hole. Lone Bear knew that to see its magic work he had to point it and pull the little leg hanging from the rifle's belly. Black Weasel had also shown him how to hold the rifle and look along the top of its barrel toward his target. They did not waste bullets test-firing it because Black Weasel said no one in the camp could make a shiny casing speak again after its spirit left its body.

Having decided to follow the column of soldiers from its backside to avoid their many eyes, Lone Bear had ridden deep to the east from the Place Where They Kill the Deer before he cut south and turned west. He urged the bay from behind a hill when he saw two Indians approaching with their mounts loaded with furs. They were poor reservation Indians going back to trade with the white men.

"I see you have chosen the easy trail that turns men into women," Lone Bear said in greeting the pair when their bony animals got to him.

"It is you, Lone Bear," the older of the two said upon recognizing the Sioux scout. "Don't be hard with us. Where we go, the white men have taken over everything. Our women sleep with them, and our children are covered with flies. The old people sit around staring into the fire to see the past. If we did not trap through the winter, we could get no meat. No one would have anything to eat."

"Our camp could always use more warriors," said Lone Bear. "Sitting Bull tells us we must fight to save our spirits and protect our hunting grounds. The white men will leave us nothing. . . . Look at you. The light in your eyes is gone. You have no arch in your back. Why can't you be men again and come with us?"

The fort Indians shrugged and moved on, their heads

sagging over their chests. They were tired, beaten men who must have eaten too much of the white man's mushy meat and drank of his crazy spirit water. The Red Way is a hard way and the White Way a wide, easy trail to follow, Lone Bear thought. His face glistened in the sunlight as he watched the two ride away.

The Sioux scout turned the bay and rode west. He headed toward a high butte the Indians called Rattlesnake Spirit Land because it was littered with the hides of the rattling ones which molted and curled together for winter in the bowels of the butte's sandstone caves. Lone Bear thought it a good lookout post for it was said the white men fear snakes as nothing else. Indians told him the white men will shoot snakes with their short or long guns. The white men had no fear of running out of bullets.

It seemed strange to Lone Bear a white man wouldn't take a forked stick and pin the snake, grab its tail, and give the crawling one a hard snap. But there was no use killing snakes all the time. They were just out there trying to live in this world, like the Indians. Rattlesnake Spirit Land would give the Sioux a wide overview of the trails that separated it from its tall brother and sister buttes farther west.

Lone Bear urged the bay from the shelter of a small stand of cottonwoods and poplar trees to cross a dry creek bed to more trees and brush. He scowled when the metallic clatter from the cavalry mount's shod hooves echoed down the dry wash channel. Sheltered from the wind, the Indian thought the sound seemed to have been made by tricky little spirit helpers.

An unseen horse ahead of Lone Bear neighed, alerting him to its presence. His horse rolled out a low snorting answer. Lone Bear leapt from his animal's back at the same instant John Benson charged.

Benson fired the Springfield's one shot at Lone Bear and missed. He drove Roman Nose toward the Indian and swung his rifle butt at him as he passed.

Lone Bear ducked and wrestled with the bay to keep it from running with the soldier's familiar horse. The Sioux raised the lever gun and fired at the white scout's back, but the bay jerked his aim off and he was wide with a point-blank shot.

He saw the soldier ram his long gun into its scabbard and pull his short gun from its holster while leaning his horse into a knee-buckling turn that kicked dust and stones high behind him.

"C'mon, you son of a skunk!" Benson yelled at the Sioux. He and Roman Nose charged straight at the Indian again.

Lone Bear grappled with the bay, which strained to join the other cavalry mount. He saw the soldier's whiskered face behind the short gun pointing at him, and he saw the face drop when the trooper's horse stumbled in a washout. The white man somersaulted through the air with the gun in one hand and his reins in the other; Lone Bear leapt to the back of his bay and ran the horse at a full gallop to the trees he was crossing toward when the incident began. Bullets whined behind him. Lone Bear pulled his horse up, drew his stone war club, and drove his moccasins deep into the animal's sides.

The big bay charged back into the open. Lone Bear bore down on the soldier who had holstered his revolver and was struggling to control his horse. The Indian's piercing war cry further startled the white's horse, and the trooper fought desperately to draw his gun while controlling the animal. Lone Bear missed the man's head with a wild swing of his club, but the heavy chunk of granite grazed his arm. He dropped the reins, and his horse trotted off snorting and stood to watch. The short barrel was back in the trooper's hand. Lone Bear flattened across his bay's back, the Indian anticipating the shots that began to chase his retreat. Only this time the Sioux kept the bay moving deeper into the trees that skirted the small battleground. The Indian looked back and saw the soldier run to his horse, mount, and begin pursuit.

Benson managed to poke a cartridge for the Springfield into his mouth and fumbled to draw the rifle from its scabbard to reload as he and Roman Nose charged the Sioux.

Lone Bear guided his mount through the trees, hit a game trail that wound around the hill, and broke out the other side onto flat ground. He heard air above him whoosh from the lead slug fired by the trooper. The bay's stride settled into a steady rhythmic pounding, and the Sioux's adrenaline built in his bloodstream.

Benson saw the gap widen between him and the retreating Indian. The trooper admitted that he was being out-ridden. As the Sioux gained ground, Benson could see the red man was heading toward cover. He reined in Roman Nose rather than give the Indian a chance to stop himself and use the captured rifle again. He watched the red man disappear behind dust.

"That slick coyote," Benson said aloud. "I thought I had him."

Lone Bear, pausing in a clump of buffalo berry bushes to look back, saw the pony soldier pull up. He nudged the bay back to a lope and marveled at its strength. The Indian scout continued his drive toward Rattlesnake Spirit Land. He had missed a chance to count coup on the white man. The pony soldier was not an easy enemy. He had courage. Lone Bear felt that Grandfather was riding with him, for the soldier had been unable to shoot more than once from his long barrel. The Indian scout believed his medicine was working.

The wind turned colder as Benson pointed Roman Nose north. He figured this Indian was dogging the column again and eventually would also head north to report back to his camp. Benson wondered where the main body was. He chuckled at the idea the Sioux might single-handedly hit the Seventh again. What a strange one. But his mirth faded at the recollection the Indian was riding his horse and carrying his gun.

The wind was building, and dark clouds were forming to the northwest. Dakota Territory was one surprising paradise, Benson thought. It must have been eighty degrees the day before. Today he warmed his cold hands on Roman Nose's neck. Benson drew on his oilskin slicker and pulled his flat-brimmed hat to his ears.

He began to think of finding a safe campsite. To return to the column and report the only Indian hostile on the prowl was the goofy horsethief who had attacked the column a few days ago didn't seem an option he had. After all, *that* Indian was dead. But if he could pick up some sign of the main body of Indians, Collins would stay off his back.

A brushy draw clinging to a bare hillside caught the army scout's eye. He reined Roman Nose up in it as the first snowflakes began falling out of a darkening sky. By the time he had the horse's saddle loosened and its halter rope staked, the wind was swirling snow over the brush and turning it white. Benson gathered dry leaves and twigs and lit a fire. He leaned back into a sandy notch eroded from the hillside and tried to warm a tin cup of water for coffee. Hunger reminded him that hardtack and beans could make a man feel great when he had nothing else to eat. The wind drove ribbons of snow across the draw. The air had cooled but still gave the scout a pleasant feeling. This was going to be a May blizzard. If he didn't panic, he was sure he could last out the storm. It pleased him to know the Indian was out there in the snowstorm, too.

Lone Bear, sensing the approach of bad weather, sought shelter after he and the bay had climbed to the top of the high butte. By the time the storm hit, they were settled in the protection of a sandstone outcrop. Three rock walls formed a cubicle that was open but sheltered from view by junipers. The Sioux could observe a wide range of prairie without either his horse or himself being seen. Only now, the entire area was washed white by snow being driven by a howling wind. Lone Bear made a fire with his flint.

Smoke from the dry cedar branches he gathered and burned filtered into his nostrils and made him feel spiritual. He began to sing his spirit song, which called on Grandfather to protect him and make him strong to endure the night. His parfleche had been loaded with pemmican. The mixture of venison, berries, and buffalo tallow gave him strength. He melted snow to drink in a gourd held above his small campfire. He longed for a warm buffalo robe to wrap himself in, but it would have slowed him. Rarely did such heavy snow come to these rolling hills in this moon when the ponies shed. He thought of it as a warning to the soldiers by Grandfather that their invasion of the great Sioux nation's hunting grounds was going bad.

As the storm built and chilled the air, Lone Bear retreated to a cave at the rear of the outcrop. He crawled back into it until the flames from his fire barely flickered into its darkness, and there he drew sand into mounds around his body before pulling juniper branches over himself. The Sioux scout's eyes closed, and his mind left the real world. In the dream world, he heard a familiar buzzing and brother rattlesnake slithered toward him. Lone Bear's spirit voice warned, "Stay calm, Lone Bear. The crawling one wants only to be warm. He will not harm you." Lone Bear remained motionless, surrendering to sleep. The storm whistled across the mouth of the cave.

CHAPTER 4

LONE Bear's eyes adjusted to the gray light touching the rim at the entrance of the cave. A crust of snow had built up on it, nearly sealing the opening. He stirred, moving deliberately to free himself from the grass and boughs covering his body, then crawled toward the light and broke out a hole big enough to exit the cave. The air was cold and brisk against his skin. Grandfather Sun was rising like a giant flower head on the horizon. The Indian clapped his arms around his ribs and rubbed his hands. His breath floated before his mouth in a little cloud. Below on the prairie, a white blanket covered what had yesterday been the brown bosom of Mother Earth. He gathered an armful of dry branches from the base of a juniper bared by wind that sculpted four-foot-high snowdrifts an arm's length from the clearing.

The Sioux entered the cave again to get more fuel from his bed of boughs. In the growing light, he saw a three-foot-long, gray limb squirm to life and slither from the body-shaped pocket he had made of sand on the cave floor. Lone Bear recalled his spirit voice. The rattlesnake, numbed by the cold, slowly made its way back into a crack at the rear wall of the cavern.

Outside, the bay horse pawed at grass peeping from the edges of drifts and nibbled the crusted snow for moisture. As the sun rose, Lone Bear scanned the land below for black spots moving in the sea of white. Nothing was visible. He ate pemmican and decided Sun would have to melt the game paths on Rattlesnake Spirit Land Butte before he could leave, so high had snow drifted.

33

John Benson, too, crawled from a snowbank that had built around his slicker-clad form during the storm. His limbs ached from the cold, but he had managed to keep his body warm. The snow had insulated him. Roman Nose stood grazing in the brush, the horse's back draped by a two-inch blanket of white through which its bay hide peered in splotches. Roman Nose's presence warmed Benson inwardly as he staggered through the drifts in search of firewood.

A cottontail rabbit jumped from a thicket and wobbled to a halt to eye the approaching trooper. Benson drew the Colt and dropped the rabbit with a head shot. He didn't care if anyone heard the shot. No one could move through the snowdrifts. The column must be mired to its haunches in problems. He skinned and gutted the small animal, then got his fire going and turned the carcass over it on a stick. The smoking meat sputtered. Benson bit a mouthful from the rabbit's leg. The body was hot from the fire under its glazed skin. Juice oozed from the corners of his mouth to his hands, and Benson saw it was blood. He bit again, quickly turning the crimson gash on the animal's leg to the fire. The meat tasted good, although his tastebuds longed for some salt. He brewed a tin cup of coffee with melted snow, drew his pipe from the saddlebag he had hanging beside his bedroll. There was no point in struggling to move out of his camp.

The storm had pinned most living things to the spot they were at when the full fury had hit. Benson feared a quick rise in temperatures would cause runoff to flood the washout he was camped in, but he hoped it would warm quickly anyway.

Benson stared at the stillness about him and wondered how anything on the open plains had survived the late spring blizzard. The wind had lumped the snow below him in the widened draw into a sea of smooth round piles.

A black speck showed on a nearby lump; then another black hole appeared on a neighbor lump. The spots popped open throughout the field of mounds, until one moved entirely, and the shaggy, black head of a buffalo bull broke through as if the earth were birthing. With the beast's stirring, the others awoke in the white world around them.

Benson was surprised to see he had been joined through the night by a herd of buffalo which had drifted to the base of his shelter in the storm. The hardy critters had crumpled into protective hairy lumps, and the snow had covered them. The draw swayed to life as the dark animals rose. Breath mist hung over them, and snorting bulls mingled their voices with bellowing calves who frolicked in the snow at their mothers' sides. It was the oddest sight Benson had ever seen. One hundred buffalo had spent the night with him.

Benson singled out a young bull that erupted from the white mass seventy-five yards from his shelter. The animal's legs buckled, and it fell to its side when the carbine slug hit its chest cavity. Blood squirted from its wound over the fresh snow. The other animals threshed and bellowed and bunched up away from Benson until leaders at the far edge found a shallow spot in the waves of snow they faced. They charged into the open, and the rest of the herd poured after them. They galloped out of sight around the curved hill.

Benson crawled to the downed animal and slit its throat, and more blood seeped from its body. The crimson stain spread beneath the animal. Benson gutted the buffalo, cut off its tongue and hump. He took the tongue and crawled back to his shelter. The sun was beginning to feel warm, and Benson decided to saddle Roman Nose to be ready to move out as the melt began. He stored the tongue in his saddlebag and crawled back to the buffalo carcass to see if he could sled the hump to his makeshift camp. The work was heavy and slow, but Benson figured the meat of the critter would be a welcome change from hardtack and salt pork. He set to work cutting the meat and hung strips out to dry over branches he laid on the snow. Benson finally sat back to smoke and watched a pair of eagles warily circle the buffalo's carcass. The scout chuckled. Eagles soaring above meant much more to Indians who thought they were holy beings than to him, who figured they were just hungry.

Lone Bear had gathered enough fuel to keep his small fire going. He crouched by it and dreamed of Little Moon. They had known each other since childhood. The scout recalled the day when he and his friends rode their imaginary ponies through the play village of Little Moon, their bare legs scattering its cottonwood-leaf tipis in a great wind. She had fastened each leaf she formed into a miniature tipi with pine needles to hold the flaps shut. Each dwelling had its opening correctly facing east. Even then, he had paused from boyish games to walk to her and touch her shoulder as she sat head bowed, sobbing over the destruction of her toy village. Then he raced off to be among his friends and continue to terrorize the women and old men of the big camp.

Little Moon had grown into a beautiful maiden and was sought by many of his tribesmen for a mate. It was rumored Sitting Bull himself had an eye for her. Little Moon had told Lone Bear many times with sly looks that she would be his some day. The scout thought he had only to distinguish himself in battle to prove his manhood to her. Although his duties as scout did not allow much time for hunting, maybe he and Little Moon could trade for enough buffalo hides to make their tipi.

It saddened him that camp tipis had to be taken down and set up again as the tribe tried to stay clear of whites and soldiers. Sitting Bull was warning the chiefs that the white man would break his word again on the Fort Laramie Treaty. Lone Bear had heard the older men saying that Sioux lands were protected by the white grandfather in the east, but that the grandfather could not control his people. The whites càme across the Missouri and made straight lines on the land and called it theirs.

This he could not understand. The world of the Sioux had no straight lines. Grandfather did not use them when he created their free world. It was apparent to Indians that the white men were willing to go against the wishes of the spirit world. Yet they professed to believe in Grandfather, whom they called God. It made little difference to the Sioux what the whites called him. Each tribe had its own word. For the Cheyenne, he was Maheo, yet the Cheyenne were their brothers. Grandfather's spirit was everywhere, breathing life and unity into both plants and animals.

Lone Bear noticed in the clearing morning air that the column of soldiers he sought was visible in the distance. They had picked a camp sheltered by round hills on all sides that his people called Home of the Yellow-Bellied Ones. It was a foolish place to be just before a big snow. Not because of the Yellow-Bellies, for they were just small four-legged weasels. The depression had filled with snow like a bowl into which broth was ladled. The soldier camp showed little movement. The horse and mule herd was bunched up on a bare side hill, swept clean by the strong wind. The soldiers' direction of movement was still pointed toward the horizon where Sun hides his light.

The Sioux scout knew he would not have more contact with soldiers that day. His thoughts turned to his own predicament.

To the north, Lone Bear saw a small herd of buffalo. He should report it to the hunters in Sitting Bull's camp. Both old and young could use a fresh supply of meat. He must find a trail leading off Rattlesnake Spirit Land. Lone Bear took sage from his parfleche and smeared his body. With outstretched arms, he wailed into the sky.

> Grandfather, take pity on me.
> I am a helpless two-legged.
> Grandfather, show me the way.
> And my heart will always be yours.

He bridled the bay horse, and they set about to find a path through the drifts that had surrounded his camp. The snow was melting as Sun drew higher above and sent warmth into Mother Earth. Game trails on the sheltered side of the butte were coated by a thin cover of snow, and Lone Bear got on his horse to move more quickly off the butte. The Indian could hear water falling from rocks. The melt was coming. It was a race.

Lone Bear knew he and the horse might plunge through the hollow crust of snow into the water of a hidden gorge. Still, he could not sit idle. The buffalo might wander too far from the camp of Sitting Bull, or worse, nearer the soldiers. The bay lost its footing and rolled from the game trail down the butte's frosted side to where the trail bent around again below. The Sioux kicked clear of the horse but lost his grip on the animal's rein. When both came up, the horse trotted away from him.

The animal would run if he chased it, so Lone Bear sat down and began to chant. The horse stopped to watch. Lone Bear slipped off the trail and crawled over a snow-filled gorge to a clump of young cottonwood trees nearly half-buried in snow. He climbed the remaining body of one tree and broke off its topmost branches. The Indian retraced his path to where the horse stood warily nibbling at a juniper tree. He ground some of the leaves and branches together and waved them slowly in the air so that the wind currents took the scent to the horse. He sat down to wait. The bay sniffed the fresh foliage and came toward

Lone Bear without coaxing. Soon the horse ate from the Indian scout's hand. The cottonwood tops rivaled in nourishment the oats soldiers gave their horses. Lone Bear took the rein and mounted the bay, and they renewed their journey.

At the base of the craggy butte, snow melt was pouring into drainages, the water forming a swirling brown stream. Lone Bear's path was blocked unless he retreated back up the slope. He slipped from the horse's back and tied his buckskins and weapons in a bundle. Grasping the horse's tail, he forced the animal into the water. The bay's body floated when its legs left solid footing, and it pushed off, stroking mightily for the opposite bank. Lone Bear clung to its tail and held the bundle above his head with his free hand. The current turned the horse's head upstream, and it swam in a sidewise gliding motion. Lone Bear felt his feet slip into a mass of underwater branches. The tree trunk's impact against his midriff doubled him over. The bay slipped from his grasp, and his bundle floated downstream.

The Sioux dove through the dark, icy water. He fought to free his right foot, which was lodged in a fork of the limbs. The current pressed hard against him in the dimness, and he bobbed to the surface for more breath. He gulped air through his nose and mouth before the current sucked him under again. Stroking hard to dive deep, he shifted the pressure on his foot which broke free. He pushed upward, his lungs begging for air. The torrent slammed him against the bank, and with his last strength, Lone Bear snagged a clump of sagebrush bent over the water. He pulled himself forward over the brush to his waist, then lost consciousness as his legs waved like underwater plants swaying to the rhythm of the water.

Lone Bear could only guess at how long he had clung unconscious to the sage, but when he awoke his legs were pressed into the muddy bank. A dam of driftwood downstream had broken and drained the gorge that had trapped him. The bay stood off a few yards. Naked and cold, the Sioux scout forced himself to approach the animal, standing transfixed near his crawling form. The rein dangled in front of the bay, which edged away from Lone Bear. He spoke softly and touched the bay's hind-quarters. The animal quivered and raised a leg protectively, but Lone Bear soothed the horse and ran his hand along its belly. The Indian moved his arm under the bay's neck and grasped the hackamore. The animal's warm body radiated heat into the naked Indian as he pulled himself on its back.

They renewed their trek, ambling almost in circles at times. They picked their way along the drainage in search of spots where the swirling storm wind had laid only a thin layer of snow on the ground. Hunger tore at Lone Bear's mind and body, but the hunger for his lost rifle ripped at his soul.

Benson loaded his meat on Roman Nose and led the big horse through the snow. The air was clear and the sky brilliant blue. The sun was melting the topmost cover, and each step the man and animal took plunged them deep into the drifts. Their tracks were black holes behind them. Their grunting and panting echoed in the stillness. The army scout aimed for the spot where the buffalo carcass lay, the eagles tearing beakfuls of meat from where they clutched it with giant yellow claws. The man and horse paused to rest after lurching forward a few steps. Both were wet from a combination of melting snow and sweat.

This is May, Benson thought. A late storm like this could put a cattleman right out of business. He tried to imagine what he would have done if he had picked this lonely spot for a ranch. Forget it. Nothing except buffalo could handle such a wintry blast. How had they survived?

A missionary had called the buffalo the devil's own

creation. Said you could tell from their curved horns and shaggy beards—they were the spitting image of Satan. Benson, heaving for more air and feeling the wetness clean through his clothing and boots, allowed the devil had made one tough creation if the missionary was right. If he and Roman Nose could just make it to the dead animal lying motionless before them, they could pick up the trail of the buffalo herd and get on to some less treacherous high ground. Water wriggling along the drainage revealed its course under the snow wherever it gurgled to the surface.

The eagles hopped from their meal as the man and horse drew nearer until the predators were overcome by fear and soared off. Roman Nose came up shivering and breathing hard when Benson gave a final tug on the reins to bring the horse to solid footing. The two rested by the dead bull. The scout tried to blot the gore of the sight from his thoughts. "It was you or me, fella," Benson said aloud. He tightened the cinch on his military saddle and got on Roman Nose to follow the trail of hoof marks already imprinted in the drifts. The eagle pair swooped lower to the buffalo carcass.

When Benson and Roman Nose rounded the hillside, the scout could see the herd had blazed a winding trail that could be easily followed to more open ground.

Lone Bear's eyes filled with tears when he miraculously found his rawhide bundle lodged in a brush pile, which surfaced as the flooding water receded. His hands tore at the package to free its contents. The rifle was not even muddy, but it needed drying. His shiny cartridges, arrows, bow, and shield, all intact. Lone Bear's thoughts rose in thanks to Grandfather.

CHAPTER 5

BENSON followed the highway built through the snowdrifts by the buffalo for five miles before he heard the first shot ahead of him.

He pulled Roman Nose into a stand of brush. The scout feared he had run into a Sioux hunting party. As he sat listening, the firing increased and continued at a steady pace.

By the time Benson edged Roman Nose out of hiding and through the saddle between hilltops he had approached, the fusillade was waning. From his vantage point, the army scout could look down to a flat onto which the fleeing buffalo had trapped themselves.

Ahead of them lay a ridge of huge snowdrifts. Their retreat had been cut off by a party of five white men.

The convulsing bodies of the downed shaggy beasts smeared blood onto the snow in a giant grotesque circle. The bellowing survivors threshed about on top of one another, leaping for freedom through the deep snow.

By the time Benson rode to the buffalo hunters, they were moving like cloaked vampires from carcass to carcass and cutting out tongues.

They tossed the steaming chunks of meat into a burlap bag before moving on to the next animal.

"We hit the bonanza, trooper," a bearded man said, dropping his rifle barrel when he recognized Benson's military uniform.

"Did you have to kill them all?" Benson said, his voiced tinged with disgust.

The smell of death hung in the air. An occasional shot

slammed dully into the kicking body of an animal still moving as the other four men waded through the carnage, slashing into the buffalos' reddened heads. The animals stared back in silence with gaping dark holes in their mouths.

"We're just doing our duty, same as you," the bearded man said, drawing a piece of paper from his greatcoat and handing it to Benson. "This is an order signed by the army commandant at Fort Rice."

Benson read the paper signed by General Stanley, which authorized the hunters to slaughter buffalo. Leave it to himself to sign on with an outfit ordered out to protect railroad surveyors and buffalo whackers.

"The word is out," the man said. "The army wants to cut the hostile Indians' supply train, and these critters are what makes it possible for them to keep raising hell. We'll have a small fortune by the time we get these animals skinned."

Benson shook his head. The stench of death rose like a cloud over the downed bodies.

"We really lucked out," the bearded man said. "They wandered right past our camp. We got 'em surrounded before they knew what was going on. What's the matter with you? You some kind of Indian lover?"

Benson said nothing. He gave him back the order, turned Roman Nose, retraced his route to the saddle, and put the ridge between himself and the dead animals. He decided to pick a muddy trail toward the westerly direction of the troop column. The hunters had shot away any possibility that Indians would be hanging around for supplies.

Lone Bear watched as Benson's lone form retreated from the carnage the hunters had wreaked on the buffalo herd. Grandfather, who had given life to all things, must be weeping. The Sioux scout had dried out his outfit and had hoped to report the Indian camp's meager meat stocks could be renewed from the herd. Anger rose in his breast, and he turned the bay back from the sight. He would skirt the valley of death and head back for Sitting Bull's camp. Sun's warmth was shrinking the snow piles, and water was running down hillsides and forming swirling pools on the flats before crawling away in snakelike patterns in dry creek beds, now running full in their banks. Warbling meadowlarks tried to cheer the bright May day, but Lone Bear's hate of whites made his thoughts bad.

He returned to the camp. Black Weasel rode out to meet his nephew when he learned that guards were flashing their mirrors to herald his return.

"What is it, my nephew?" the older Indian said in greeting. "Your face tells me you have angry thoughts. You survived the last puff of breath from our grandfather to the north. You must be thankful for that."

The two rode slowly into camp. Lone Bear, tired and hungry, appreciated the silence his uncle permitted him. After they turned their horses out, Lone Bear told of his experiences. His uncle nodded his approval during the narrative until the scout gave the news of the buffalo slaughter. The older Indian left Lone Bear to rest and went to summon the camp chiefs. They would form a war party to avenge the wasteful massacre of the great beasts.

Lone Bear, lying on a fur robe in his uncle's tipi, saw Little Moon stroll past the opening. She was shrouded in a sea of blue sky. The Indian maiden looked shyly toward him, but he was sure she couldn't see him in the dimness of his shelter.

His eyelids closed heavily, and his mind joined the spirit world of dreams. He saw his people rejoicing at the return of their hunters, pack animals heavily ladened with bulky bundles of juicy buffalo meat. The people danced to a vibrant drumbeat. Little children played stick games and ran forward to catch tidbits cast to them by the triumphant hunters. The world of the Sioux was a thing of beauty given by Grandfather for all to share.

When Lone Bear awoke, the camp was still. He crawled from his bed and pushed open the tipi flaps. Sun was painting the horizon pink and orange, and the Daybreak Star bid his eyes a glowing welcome from a sea of black which melted first into deep blue, lightening in hue as it flowed toward the dark silhouette of the hills.

The moment touched the Indian scout's inside spirit, and he felt moved to go out and talk to Grandfather. He picked a nearby rock cliff where air currents freshened and swirled about him. He rubbed his body with sage from a small pouch attached to his breechcloth.

Alone, overlooking the quiet camp below, Lone Bear stretched forth his arms, and facing east, he called on Grandfather to hear him. To remember that hard times had come to his people. That the people needed food and good shelter. That the white man needed his eyes opened to see the harm he was causing. The scout prayed for the peace path.

But even as he prayed and the sun spread its light into the deep shadows of the landscape, Lone Bear saw in the distance the slow-moving forms of warriors returning to the camp. He hiked back to the valley floor upon which lodges had been pitched in a great circle.

Black Weasel was among the men who rode silently. He carried a lance tipped by a fresh scalp. Lone Bear strode to meet his uncle. The slaughter of the buffalo had been avenged. He took the rein of Black Weasel's horse when the elder Indian slipped from its back at the entrance to his tipi. Black Weasel drove the lance shaft into the ground, and the bloody tuft of hair swirled around the pole, finally dangling motionless.

When Lone Bear returned from pasturing his uncle's pony with the rest of the camp herd, Black Weasel was eating from a bowl of hash. The older Indian brought forth his pipe and filled it with tobacco flakes from one of the small cloth sacks bartered for from their French trader friend Beneteu.

"We surprised the whites as they were stacking hides they had taken from the bodies of our brother buffalo," Black Weasel told the scout. "We swept down on them before they knew what was happening. We killed two men, and three got away on their fast horses. One carried an arrow in his side."

Lone Bear knew then that camp would be broken that day. The Indians feared the soldiers would be told and that an attack would be launched against them. Game was already thinning at the Place Where They Kill the Deer. They dared not move south, so the trek would be made farther west and north along the small river. Ahead on the prairie, the Indians hoped to find buffalo. Young men would want to release their anger by attacking any of the white man's wagons. The wagons carried food, and the whites were always good for a handful of new horses or mules.

Sun was high in the sky, and despite the strain of another move under fear of an attack, the spring day itself was cheery and fresh. Lodge poles were struck swiftly and silently. The camp moved out in unison behind leaders. By clinging to the ridge backs wherever possible, the Indians were able to move across prairie grass neither blocked by snowdrifts, nor soggy with mud. The people slogged on, leaving a winding black trail across the flats whenever they were forced from the ridges.

Lone Bear rode his bay horse at the side of Little Moon's spotted pony, whose travois pulled part of her family's belongings. Her widowed mother and little brother were afoot, the mother leading a stolen army mule laden with rawhide bundles and tugging the skins of their small lodge on the crossed lodge poles trailing behind the animal. The youth was flanked by a pair of dogs, each also burdened with camp supplies on small travois.

"How long can we continue to run like this, Lone Bear?" the young woman said. Her face, though defiantly beautiful, was beginning to show a hardness of greater years.

Lone Bear's heart was alive in her presence. "The chiefs say we will run when it is wise and strike when the white men grow tired of the chase. The whites are slow to learn, but before the end we may make them understand our ways."

"The old women say the whites have no spirit helpers. Nothing to hold their hands from taking up the long guns."

"Then, we must have more of these," said Lone Bear, gripping his lever gun strongly where it rested across his bone saddle.

She smiled at his resolve, but doubts nagged her thoughts of Lone Bear as a potential partner. He had no family closer than Black Weasel and few belongings because he was a scout, always going out alone. But he was lean and bronze, his mind was straight, and he had proved to be brave and strong. Little Moon wondered if he would ever find courage to ask her mother for her hand as mate. What gift could he bring for her? She warmed to the thought of lying by his side on a thick buffalo robe, their fire crackling softly at their feet.

Her reverie was interrupted by loud shouting on the trail before them. Lone Bear dug his moccasins deep into the bay and charged forward. A low growl erupted from a clump of bushes off the trail, muffling the wail of an old woman, who had slipped from the column to relieve herself. It was grizzly bear's voice. The bear dragged the moaning woman through the undergrowth.

Lone Bear leapt from his horse's back, gripping his lever gun in his right hand. He ran toward the hole in the dense brush into which the bear and woman had vanished. The old one's voice was weakening as he broke through the undergrowth following the fading sound. The huge female bear was hunched like a giant furry ball over the form of the old woman, who was lying still on the ground when Lone Bear got to them.

Upon hearing the noise he made, the she-bear looked up, its small dark eyes glistening when its nose caught his scent. The bear rose on its hind legs and towered above the body of the old woman, then came down on all fours and charged Lone Bear. He dropped to one knee and pointed the lever gun. The bear's head bobbed as it charged. Lone Bear's rifle rose and fell with the movement. He sought to hit the bear just over the nose in the forehead. The Indian saw the bear spring from the ground toward him. He squeezed the trigger and rolled away at the blast from the bullet. The bear's wind, even its fur, brushed his body as it drove past. Lone Bear came to his feet and ran toward the shape of the old woman before he whirled and faced the animal again, his knife drawn.

The she-bear's body threshed in the thicket. Lone Bear felt the ground tremble beneath his feet, the branches and vines vibrating at the spot where the bear was convulsing. He tensed, waiting for the animal to rise and charge again. The quaking brush calmed. The bear's death moan was the last sound before quiet.

Lone Bear, taking time to reload a shell into the lever gun, stooped to gently shake the old woman. She was lifeless, her face and skull smashed by the fangs of the bear. Men's excited voices grew louder. Lone Bear looked up to see Black Weasel leap into the clearing, muzzle-loader ready to be cocked and fired. The warriors bunched up around him before lifting the body of the woman and carrying it back to the column. She was a widow, whose body had grown bony from neglect and loneliness.

Lone Bear moved with his uncle to the spot where the bear had fallen. A bad odor drifted from the animal, but the two men came to it and poked the form with their gun barrels. No movement. Shattered bone fragments and flesh oozed with blood from the rear of the bear's huge head. Lone Bear's bullet had entered just to the right of the ridge of the bear's nose at the skull's weak spot. Black Weasel helped his nephew cut the bear's claws from its feet.

"You have taken the spirit of this great beast," his uncle said as they worked over the downed hulk. "You now truly have the bear power, a strength most warriors never get. The elders were right when they told of your vision dream about a great single bear roaming alone through the land. From the dream, you were named Lone Bear."

The younger Indian hid his feelings, but his heart was warm with pride. He would thread one claw on a strip of rawhide for a necklace and give the others to his uncle who could make gifts of them. The two men withdrew from the bear's odor to let others reenter the lair and butcher the animal. There would be meat and feasting in camp tonight, and the council of chiefs and headmen would hear from Black Weasel about the great courage of Lone Bear, who had earned the full right to his name.

Little Moon was relieved when she saw the young scout climb on the back of his bay and ride toward her. The people resumed pace to catch up with the lead elements of the column, unaware of the fight.

John Benson rode slowly toward the black figure of Isaiah Dorman, who was trying to cut his mules out of the milling horse herd. The animals were meandering through melting snow to nibble at grass that was being bared by the sun.

Troopers caught in the drifts built in the bowl they had used for a campsite were cursing and struggling to free themselves. Blue shirts and trousers fluttered from poles where they had been hung to dry.

"Howdy, friend," Benson said, nodding to Dorman. "You have any idea where Collins is in this mess?"

"Howdy yourself, John Benson," Dorman said, pausing from tugging on the lead rope attached to a stubborn mule. "You sure don't look none the worse for that snowstorm."

"I got a little something that might warm your insides," Benson said. He dropped from Roman Nose, dug the buffalo meat from his saddlebags, and handed it to Dorman. "Tuck this away in one of those satchels of yours, Isaiah."

"Sergeant Collins is down there by the general's tent somewhere. He's been running around shouting like it was our fault it snowed."

Benson turned Roman Nose loose with the other animals and trudged through the mixture of wet snow and mud toward the big tent.

"How did you survive?" Collins said when the scout came up. "I bet we lost you in the blizzard."

"Sorry to disappoint you," Benson said.

"Find any more Indians?"

"I had a run-in with one, who was riding a bay army horse and carrying a Winchester," the scout said wryly. "We were eyeball to eyeball, but he wouldn't stand and fight," Benson said.

Collins didn't press the scout for a more descriptive report. But the sergeant grew excited when he learned of the slaughter of the buffalo herd.

"If there's any Sioux whooping around out there, that ought to get their dander up. We'll find 'em and whip 'em yet," the sergeant said.

The disarray of everything in the soggy camp cut short Collins's usual robust curiosity. He advised Benson to get some chow and rest and be ready to go out again when the column regained its freedom.

Benson found Dorman with his mules strung together ready to be packed. He had built a small fire and was roasting buffalo steaks from which he had neatly trimmed the soiled outer crust.

"Care for some coffee, John Benson?" Dorman said.

"Isaiah, I haven't heard such sweet words in a long time. I hope you aren't planning to hog all that meat."

"I cooked enough for two. If word gets around we are eating this high on the hog, we may have company."

"Let's get busy, then," said Benson, cutting an end off a chunk of the roasting meat.

The two men squatted by the fire to keep their rear ends from getting soggy. Dorman said the general had handpicked the campsite and ordered men to guard the tops of surrounding hills to protect against attacks by hostiles. Word was the general had likened the spot to a medieval castle with guards on the walls. It turned out to be a windless bowl into which the storm ladled snow. The storm had driven the ridge defenders back into camp. And the snow piled up all around them. Now, with the sun heating up, moving to the edges was a slog through a cold, muddy mess.

"One thing a man learns sooner or later in this country is not to trust low spots," said the black man.

"I wonder whether the Indian survived the storm," the scout said to Dorman.

"Wouldn't have thought anyone but a damned fool would be riding out there in that snow," Dorman replied. "Even the badgers stay in their holes when the old north wind howls this late in the year."

"Isaiah, you wouldn't have believed it. Here comes that supposed-to-be-dead Indian, clattering along louder than me and Roman Nose. The metal shoes on that horse he stole from me tipped his whereabouts long before he got near me. So I just set up my ambush and almost got him. We skirmished. He stayed lucky and got away on that fast bay."

Dorman reckoned the Indian would do what horse troopers were not allowed to do. The shoes would drop off the stolen horse and never be put back on again by a camp farrier.

"Those Sioux told me long ago they figured the Great Spirit favored them over the white man. Whenever there was soldiers trying to sneak up on them, the little spirit helpers told the Indians by making the clinking sounds."

"Well, this time I managed to sneak up on him," said Benson.

"I hope he isn't a relative of mine. I told my woman I was hiring out so we could stock a piece of land near her Santee people," said the black man. "More coffee?"

"Thanks."

"You know, I can't say I'm sorry the Indian got away, but I'm glad you come through it okay. I got a growing fondness for you, John Benson."

"You're gettin' a little on the gentle side to be riding with an outfit like this, ain't you?"

"Maybe. But if you take a paintbrush and paint everybody the same color in your own mind, John Benson, you'd be surprised at how it changes your attitude. Some people never do find time to do that in their whole life."

The word was passed along to Dorman and Benson that because of the snow they would camp here for another night. The command was advised to move tents outward on the perimeter to avoid more disaster. Dorman led his mules back to the horse herd. Some troopers rode out toward a bunch of antelope seen moving from the flat land into the mouth of a box canyon sandwiched between a pair of huge buttes. Reports of their rifles echoed back to camp just after the soldiers and their mounts disappeared as dark specks bobbing into the canyon's mouth.

Benson was overcome by fatigue. He crawled into the tarp he shared with Dorman, left even his boots on, and slept deeply.

In the haze of his dreams, Benson heard Sergeant Collins's loud voice.

"Where's Benson? Benson, get out here, on the double. C'mon, get out of that sack."

By the time the scout got his eyes to open, Collins had

his head stuck in the tent. Benson's left boot grazed the sergeant's chin as the scout rolled quickly, came to his knees, and grabbed the Colt hanging from the tent pole near his head.

The hammer cracking back to full cock split the silence, and the barrel's dark hole stared deadly at a point between Collins's blue eyes.

"Don't shoot, Benson! It's me, Collins, you jackass."

Benson feigned surprise and dropped the hammer. "I thought you were a Sioux. Shouldn't sneak up on a man like that."

"You crazy. You shoot me, and you'll spend the rest of your life in the stockade."

"Sorry, Sergeant. A man gets a little edgy."

Collins said three buffalo hunters had hit camp, one wounded. They had been attacked by Indians, who killed two of their party. "The general wants a detail to recover the bodies and engage the Indians if they are still around. The hunters said there was about twenty.

"And they said a trooper had visited their camp before the attack."

Benson explained he had trailed the herd in hopes of spying on Indian hunters who might have come to prey on the big critters. But he had moved on when the white men decimated the buffalo herd.

"Bad news travels just as fast to Indians as it does anywhere else, I guess," the scout said.

"Get ready to saddle up," Collins said. The sergeant left to pick a detail of fifty troopers.

"John Benson, you sure like to take big risks with your life, playing a trick on a man like Sergeant Collins."

"If I had pulled the trigger, Isaiah, at least I wouldn't have to spend the next couple of days with him. I took this scouting duty just to stay away from the likes of him."

Dorman rose to make breakfast while Benson got Roman Nose ready. Dark blotches of brown had been bared in the snow by the full warmth of yesterday's sunshine.

CHAPTER 6

THE troopers and Private John Benson first saw the circling eagles and hawks. Below them, magpies mixed with the bigger birds, all fluttering from one dark patch to another. As the men approached the buffalo hunters' camp, they saw coyotes nipping and snarling and tugging at chunks of food. A dozen wolves fled from the carnage when the soldiers rode up.

At the perimeter of where the bunched-up buffalo had been taken down by a hail of lead, the bodies of two hunters lay crumpled in a heap of mud, snow, and their own blood.

The officer ordered a detail of guards out to protect the grisly work ahead of the soldiers.

"Recognize anybody?" Collins asked Benson.

"That big guy with the beard. I talked to him. He had an order from Fort Rice that permitted this."

Four soldiers grunted as they extracted the stiff body from its mud-caked tomb. One of the big man's arms had hardened into a hook where it had fallen over the neck of a dead buffalo the victim had tried to hide behind during the attack.

The bodies had been stripped and the guns and ammunition taken. Deep red patches on their skulls revealed they had been scalped.

"We'll make those redskins pay for this, Benson," the sergeant said grimly. "When the general finds out, they can sell their souls. The rest belongs to us."

Collins rode with the scout to high ground from which the Indians had launched their attack. Apparently, the distance between bodies showed the warriors had made a successful surprise raid. The Sioux had fanned out behind the ridge and charged.

Benson watched the soldiers strap the hunters' bodies to the backs of pack animals. It seemed a terrible waste to him. Two men dead, all for so much buffalo meat and hides that were now rotting in the sun. There was no winner, except maybe the ranting Collins. Or maybe the general would become a winner, once he got the details and avenged the deaths.

"Scavengers," the scout said.

"What are you mumbling about, Benson?" Collins said as the two rode back to the main party.

"I said, scavengers. Two legged and four—nothing but a heap of carrion eaters."

"I suppose you thought being a cavalry trooper was a milk and honey trip?"

"No, Sergeant. I just wanted to see the big, beautiful West. I'd have settled for sunsets."

"Benson, you're a sad case. We're out here to kill hostile Indians and protect white people, not look at sunsets. What are you complaining about, anyway? Do you know why I got you scouting? Because you're good at it, but the other reason is you don't get on good with people, Benson. If it wasn't for people like us killing enough of them redskins, there wouldn't be room out here for people like you."

The sergeant's sermonizing in the midst of so much human error angered the scout.

But he was right. Private John Benson had come West because he wanted land for a ranch. He was no more concerned about what happened to Indians and hide hunters than he was about what was going on back East.

"We'll take these poor devils back to our camp and see they get a decent burial," Collins said. "You've been out a long time without a good rest, Benson, but I want you to pick up the trail of the hostiles and get us a report on where we can hit them."

That lifted some of the gloom off Benson's thoughts. As weary as he was, he was glad to be leaving the troop. The ride back was likely to be sullen as they carted the two dead white men. For some of the troopers, it was their first encounter with death. No doubt, some of the old hands would break them in with horror stories of Indian atrocities.

"I'll do my best, Sergeant," Benson told Collins. The scout turned Roman Nose away from the column forming up to move out.

"Watch your hair."

"I'll watch my hair and a lot more," Benson replied. The scout followed the hoof marks left by the retreating war party back to the high ground. The warriors had split into two groups, and Benson slumped in his saddle while he gave the sign some thought. Somewhere to the north was their camp. The groups would eventually meet there. The army scout decided to ride straight, following neither trail. At some point, he could head east or west and hit their tracks again. And if they were watching their backtrail, he wouldn't be on it.

Benson rode the midsections of hills, dismounting and slowly checking afoot before passing to the other side. He crossed the shortest distance over flats between high spots and tried to follow cover. Gullies were still too muddy for travel. The sun was back to full strength, and the wind was sweeping moisture from the prairie.

Finding a suitable camp was the second most important thing on his mind behind not being surprised by the marauding Indians.

The wind built to a fluctuating low roar, and he and Roman Nose leaned toward the northwest. The horse's mane and tail streamed off easterly, and Benson's hatbrim flopped back over the crown, then snapped back to slap him across the eyes. It was annoying, so the scout took off his hat and crammed it inside his shirt. Before long, the sun was burning his head and he put the hat back on, tugging it down to his ears. He overcame a desire to stick Roman Nose with the round ends of his cavalry spurs and roar off across the prairie hollering at the sky. The wind was maddening.

Then Benson thought of Isaiah Dorman's advice. "Don't fight that strong wind out there. The animals don't. They just pick a spot to lie down and wait it out."

The scout pulled Roman Nose into a clump of buffalo brush, dismounted, and loosened the saddle. He slipped the bridle out of the animal's mouth and let it graze at the end of its halter rope. Benson found a niche of sandstone that was out of the wind and sat down to smoke his pipe and chew on a chunk of buffalo. He thought of women he had known, women he had slept with. The scout thought any one of them would be a welcome companion right now.

Roman Nose let out a low, frightened rumble and shied to break loose from the tether. Benson came quickly to his feet, Colt whipped out, adrenaline pumping through his body. The mountain lion left the ground in a giant leap toward the horse at the same instant the gun fired. The shot missed but disrupted the cat's course. The animal hit the ground and whirled to hiss at Benson as the second round left the gun barrel. The slug caught the tawny beast at the right shoulder and dug into its chest cavity. The cat rolled into a pulsating lump that Benson quickly stilled with another shot into its head. He calmed the horse and moved it away from where the carcass lay, but Roman Nose was hunched up and trembling.

"All right, you old buzzard," Benson said, "have it your way. That big pussycat surprised me, too." He tightened the saddle cinch and slipped the bit back in the horse's mouth. They again headed onto the open hillside, and

Benson tried to ignore the wind. The scout figured he could have skinned the cat and traded its hide to some officer. But he knew Roman Nose would rather not get stuck hauling the smelly bundle. "C'mon, settle down, you old sodbuster," Benson said gently to the horse.

They stuck to the northerly course until Benson saw the skyline broken ahead by a range of towering buttes. It was as if nature had paused to rest on the spot to survey all of the surrounding land which it had rearranged into rolling hills and flat lands. The buttes relieved his eyes from the monotony. Brush and trees darkened the high ravines along a five-mile southern exposure. Benson suspected that he had come upon the place where the Indians were making their home, but from the distance he could not detect any movement. He opted to camp without making a fire and check out the buttes in the morning.

Lone Bear's people had moved into a basin of dried grass overlooking the small, winding river that emptied into its big brother river, which sliced through Sioux hunting grounds.

The land was rugged and small game abundant. Beaver lodges dotted the stream, and the tracks of many deer showed in the sand where they had come to stand and drink. Juniper trees and sage gave a rich aroma to the air, which mixed in the smoke from campfires built of cedar.

After helping Little Moon's mother assemble the family's small tipi, Lone Bear had slipped away from the camp to walk with the young maiden along the banks of the small river. She paused as they strolled to root out turnips with her digging stick. Mother Earth had stored the small vegetables under her earth mantle through the winter.

"This is for you," she said, laughing and pressing into his hand one of the small tubers she had dipped in the water.

"Little Moon. I have more on my mind than child's

games," he said. "You and I have grown up. Do you ever think of taking a man?"

She smiled. "He would have to be very brave. He would have to be able to go out into the land by himself and not be frightened by spirits and animals."

"Would he be anything like me?"

"I think so. But I would not like a man who has so serious an attitude as you have. My mother says I should look for an older man. But they seldom smile, even when times are good."

"Maybe you should marry the people's clown. He is always laughing and jumping around."

"I would think very seriously about marrying a young man who has a good, strong heart."

"You know that I have little to offer your mother as gifts because I am a scout."

"We have grown accustomed to living on little since the pony soldiers killed my father many winters ago." Lone Bear remembered. His own family had been wiped out in the same battle by the rolling guns. He, a small boy, had been taken in by the family of Black Weasel when the tribe had retreated along the same route they had just come. That was the year of the crippled warrior's death and the destruction of most of the tribe's winter supplies. It was, they say, the time when Sitting Bull's heart turned to stone against the whites. The battle of the Place Where They Kill the Deer was started when the pony soldiers fired on the lame man.

The Man Who Never Walked had come to Sitting Bull, they say, to plead for the right to fight and die like a warrior. The Indians made him a travois and watched from the hilltops when the lame one rode forth behind his war pony to challenge the soldiers. They were spread out below the Indian camp. They shot the crippled man while he rode before them singing his death song. From that time, it is said, Sitting Bull knew the white men had no heart when it came to red men.

"I will bring your mother a gift for your hand," Lone Bear said softly to Little Moon.

"I will be waiting, Lone Bear." They returned to camp, and the Indian scout made preparations to go out again. The chiefs warned that the camp must be ever vigilant. The white soldiers were riding just one or two days south and could make a quick attack on the Indians.

When Benson awoke, he carefully checked the long range of buttes for movement. Seeing none, he saddled Roman Nose and headed for the high peak on the eastern edge. He still clung to the midsection of hills, working his way slowly through saddles and watching for any sign of human activity.

The first sign came when Roman Nose tugged at the reins to trot forward to water. A clear, meandering creek hidden beneath its carved banks had given its presence away to the thirsty horse's nostrils. Benson dismounted to fill his canteen while the horse drank. The scout found the fresh tracks of Indian ponies. He reckoned it was the sign of half of the raiders. The tracks led off from the creek toward the midway point of the long range of buttes. Benson was certain it was where the main body of Indians was. He figured that must be the spot where General Alfred Sully had pounded them twelve years earlier. It had to be the Killdeer Mountains. No other land without buffalo could support a large number of Indians.

Benson headed out toward the easternmost point of the ridge of buttes and pushed Roman Nose to a lope across a stretch of flat land. The scout suspected that the area he was entering was deserted. He found a trail leading up the steep slopes, dismounted, and led his horse. When they reached the summit, the view was expansive. The plateau stretched to the west. The southern prairie sprawled below.

Benson followed the ridge. Roman Nose acted up again

when they came to a plume of steam rising into the air. The scout dropped from his horse's back with his Springfield in hand and crept along rocks toward the misty column. He strained to look over a rock ledge, and below he saw the black mouth of a cave. Around the hole were tied ribbons of tobacco. It appeared to be an Indian shrine, but it was deserted. Benson felt uncomfortable in the eerie setting. Farther along the flat tops, the scout saw pony tracks and matted grass. On a wide stretch of bare ground below, black spots dotted the landscape, marks left by campfires that had glowed by the Indians' tipis. It was quiet. The scout rode on until he came to the large trail the Indians left when they moved west. He guessed five hundred people may have been in the camp.

Benson figured the Indians were headed for the Little Missouri River, or even the Missouri itself. He could ride south to find the Seventh and report what he suspected. Collins would be satisfied. The size of the Indian encampment would prohibit sending out a small detachment to avenge the hunters' deaths. General Stanley had been following his marching orders to proceed west from Bismarck with the surveyors to follow the Yellowstone. The incident with the hunters could be neatly tucked away in a report.

Movement down on the prairie caught Benson's eye. Three wagons topped by grayed canvas and flanked by two riders were jostling their way on a westerly course. There goes another bunch of crazies bent on settling in paradise, the scout thought. He rode down off the slopes of the buttes and headed straight for the small wagon train. As he neared them, the two riders pulled away from the wagons to block his approach. The older man carried a double-barreled shotgun, the youth a small-bore rifle.

"Don't come any closer," the older man said as Benson trotted Roman Nose toward them.

"Have no fear, friend, I am a scout with the U.S. Army. Aren't you folks a little far off the beaten path?"

"Pa, he is an army man. I can see the yellow stripe on his blue pants leg," the boy said.

They laid their guns down sideways over their saddles and welcomed Benson. The scout learned they had been bound by steamboat on the Missouri River for Fort Benton, but the boat had pulled out without them while the older man's sick wife was doctored. When she recovered, they bought wagons to strike out on their own to complete their journey.

"Care to join us for some vittles?" the older man said. "We haven't eaten since breaking camp early this morning."

They bunched the wagons, and the youth got firewood. There were three families. They had been caught in the blizzard but had been prepared for bad weather. They were from upper Michigan, bound for Fort Benton to open businesses.

A young, blond woman and an older lady moved about the kettle quickly set to simmering over the fire.

"Emmy Lou, Sarah, come over here and meet our guest."

Benson doffed his hat and had trouble convincing his eyes it wasn't polite to stare. The younger woman's pale blue eyes met his and dropped shyly after she said, "Emmy Lou Farley. So nice to meet you."

Her woven-wool pantlegs dropped gracefully from a sheepskin jacket that cloaked a plaid shirt. She was slim, but she was wiry and didn't look out of place. The settlers showed confidence Benson didn't want to destroy. The scout guessed the couple were in their fifties, their daughter in her mid-twenties, the son, maybe sixteen.

"Emmy Lou decided to come with us after her husband died last winter. They were married less than a year," said the older man, who gave his name as Seth Harris.

Benson's appetite was robust. The two women handed out plates of baked beans, sliced ham, and boiled potatoes.

The fare included sourdough rolls they had baked in a Dutch oven and covered with honey, as well as hot, black coffee. When the group finished eating, one of the other wagoneers broke out a harmonica and played "Old Susannah." Everyone clapped and laughed, and for that short time the hardships of crossing the plains were forgotten.

Benson warned the settlers of the trouble with Indians. He said he'd be scouting ahead and would let them know how bad things were if they insisted on heading West.

Before he and Roman Nose rode away, the scout stopped to say good-bye to Emmy Lou.

"A pleasure meeting you, ma'am. Would you mind if I paid my respects in Fort Benton if I get over that way?"

"By all means do," she replied.

Benson felt protective of the woman but knew fate dealt the cards. His job was to locate the Indian camp and report on it. The settlers would have been better off traveling with a bigger wagon train. But the lure of the new land stirred souls to folly. He headed to pick up the Indian trail. The weather had warmed, flowers were dancing in the wind, and the land was drying.

CHAPTER 7

LONE Bear was happy as he rode out to gather information for his chiefs. He would find a gift for Little Moon's mother. Had the white men not killed the buffalo, maybe he could have brought in meat and a buffalo robe. Better to steal another fine army mule. The whites had plenty. If they were brave, they could come against the Sioux warriors and take some back. The mules were good, strong animals, taking easily to carrying packs of the camp's supplies.

He rode south along the winding little river, crossing open land when he was forced to leave the cottonwoods that grew along the riverbank curves. Small groups of deer came erect at his approach, then skipped into brush. Protected from the wind by the hills flanking the river, Lone Bear and the bay enjoyed the sun's warmth. They paused to watch a badger chuck dirt through its rear legs in pursuit of a prairie dog. The rest of the village of small animals sat on their mounds and screeched at the intruder. The hungry badger ignored their anger.

A bald eagle dove to the river's surface and grabbed a fish with its talons before soaring back to the bared limbs of a tall tree. The great bird clutched the fish and pecked the water creature's head with its beak until it stopped flopping. Then the raptor spread its wings and beat toward sandstone ledges that tumbled under their weight from a gumbo hill like giant loaves of brown bread.

Lone Bear tensed at the first whiff of smoke he smelled drifting along the river channel. He dismounted and tied the bay in brush. Crouching low, he worked forward until he saw a small, smoldering fire. Five Indian ponies stood hobbled between the fire and the river. Four Indians sat crouched by the flame. They were painting their bodies. Crows, probably planning a horse raid.

A branch cracked behind him. A heavy weight dug into his back. Lone Bear's body uncoiled, dumping the Crow clawing his midsection into a hump in front of him. The enemy Indian grunted and howled a warning before Lone Bear's knife plunged into his chest.

The others sprang to their horses. Lone Bear ripped away a heavy parfleche the dead Indian had strapped over his neck and ran to his own horse. He heard the screaming Crows breaking through the brush as he swung up on his mount. He whirled the bay, and it strained to hit full stride. Lone Bear raced back along the route he had just traveled. The strong cavalry horse vibrated firmly under his body, and Lone Bear let the animal have its head. The Crow yells faded behind them.

Two of the pursuers cut across the flat of an oxbow on the river and got ahead of the retreating Sioux. They whipped their ponies around to face him, then charged, screeching war cries.

Lone Bear saw the lead Crow's horse hit a hole in the pockmarked prairie dog town and throw its rider. The other brave came on, his war club swirling over his head. The Sioux smashed his rifle butt on the Crow's shoulder, unseating him from his horse, too. His companion ran forward on the ground to meet the oncoming scout.

Lone Bear cocked the Winchester and fired its single round at the running man, who ducked as the Sioux swept past. Lone Bear pulled the bay up, fumbled for another shell, and reloaded. The two Crows on horseback flanked the man afoot and swept him from the ground. He hurled himself behind one rider, and the three broke off the pursuit and retreated to their other comrade who had remounted. They were no match for the lever gun.

Lone Bear waved the rifle defiantly, reared the bay in a circle, and charged away from the foes.

The Sioux scout rode down from a hillside to his camp after signaling that enemy raiders had been spotted upriver. A group of young boys ran to greet him when he came in and got off his horse. Lone Bear sought out his uncle, who heard his report and went to alarm the chiefs.

"You are having quite a bit of action for a scout," Black Weasel told his nephew when he returned.

"It seems to come to me," Lone Bear replied. "I took this from the Crow I killed." He handed the rawhide pack to his uncle.

The elder Indian opened the bag and dumped its contents. Seven steel knives and two of the white man's sharpening stones clanked onto the robe on which they sat.

"This is a fine treasure," said Black Weasel, drawing the blade of one of the knives over his thumb. He said the chiefs would order a war party to hit the Crows.

The scout gave one knife to his uncle before putting the remainder back in the parfleche. He had his gift for Little Moon's mother. He would bathe, rest, and confront her before scouting again.

The lithe Indian was nervous when he approached the small tipi of Little Moon. Her mother was bent over the fire, tending a metal pot of broth.

"You are too late to visit my daughter, Lone Bear. But you will find her gathering firewood at the river."

"I have come this time to talk to you, Lost Flower," he said.

"What is it you have come to say?" the older woman said, straightening and brushing her long braids back. The ropes of black and gray settled gently out of the way so she could fold her arms under her bosom. Her buckskin skirt was soiled and wearing thin.

"I have brought you these." He thrust the Crow parfleche at her and waited for a reaction.

"A gift. What could a poor scout offer anyone?" she said.

"It is all I have." Lone Bear peered at Lost Flower's face. She knelt to empty the bag's contents on the ground.

"Knives? You bring knives. We need meat, Lone Bear, not knives. We have only one young boy to hunt for a lodge of three." Lost Flower's dark eyes failed to harden as she spoke.

"They can be traded," he said, hopefully. "White man's knives have value and are easy to pack. You can use the sharpening stones and gain favors from hunters."

The knives were still lying before her mother when Little Moon returned with a bundle of firewood.

"This young man has brought a present to our lodge, I know not why," Lost Flower said. "Perhaps you and he should go for a walk, and he will explain."

When the older woman gathered the instruments together and took the parfleche into her lodge, Lone Bear knew he had won.

Little Moon did not speak until they were well away from the lodge. "She has accepted you," she said.

"She has. But what about you?"

"Lone Bear, you fool. I loved you since the day you and your friends raided my little camp of leaves. And you came back to comfort me."

"Will you be my wife?"

"We are as one."

"I will tell my uncle."

The two young people walked arm in arm to the river. When they were out of sight of the village, Lone Bear turned the young woman toward him and pressed his lips to hers. The warmth of her body flowed through him. Tonight he would enter her lodge to become the husband of Little Moon and the family's chief provider.

Benson, lying at the brow of a high butte, saw that the Indian trail ended at the Little Missouri River. A gray haze rose like a misty curtain from their campfires. The sight of one hundred lodges awed him, then caused him to worry about the wagon train. The settlers were on a course headed straight for the Indian camp. A war party of twenty braves loped into view; they were headed his way. The army scout headed Roman Nose east, ahead of the Indians. They did not seem aware of his presence but were sure to find his sign if they kept coming. Benson loped his horse across the flats until he came to another butte. He circled to the far side, dismounted, and climbed for a look at his backtrail.

He was in time to see the war party studying the tracks Roman Nose had left. The Indians talked and pointed in his direction. Half of them split off and moved south, and the other ten warriors turned on his trail and whipped up their ponies.

"Let's go, you old Roman-nosed buzzard bait," Benson said, swinging into the saddle and digging his spurs into the horse's sides.

The cavalry horse flattened out, and its hooves drummed the prairie. Benson gained on the Indians by the time they came into view at his last vantage point. They saw him, and the army scout knew he was in for a run.

The Indian ponies strung out, the fastest outdistancing the slower. The two lead warriors held their horses to the pace Benson was setting. The army scout jumped his mount over a narrow washout that wiggled unseen through the level prairie. Roman Nose's front legs buckled on impact from the jump, but Benson pulled his horse's head up and kept the animal from stumbling. The big horse stretched the lead over most of the pursuers, but the nearest pony was swift and seemed to be closing.

Benson, looking back, saw the Indian gaining. "C'mon," he said. The scout pulled the Colt.

The warrior, an arrow notched in his bow, was off guard

when Benson swung his horse and charged back at him. The arrow the Indian shot arched over the scout's head. By the time he was in pistol range, the Indian's war club was poised. Benson rode straight at him, then pulled Roman Nose up, aimed, and fired. The slug ripped into the Indian's chest and toppled him. Benson spun Roman Nose and raced away. War cries pitched higher when the others drove past their fallen comrade's body. Benson fired two rounds at them to slow them down. It was now a ride for life that stretched into miles.

The three wagons bobbed on the prairie in front of him, and Benson fired warning shots as he neared. By the time he got to them, the women occupants were lying on the ground and the men had taken positions behind the wagon boxes and wheels.

"Any more coming than these?" Seth Harris yelled to Benson as he hurled himself from his horse.

"That's all of them, but there's a lot more where they came from," the scout replied, tossing his saddlebag with ammunition on the ground in front of him. Benson laid the Colt and a pile of bullets beside each other and built another mound of cartridges for the Springfield.

"Wait till they get in close," he yelled down the short line of wagons.

Benson put his rifle sights on the lead warrior, but the Indian leaned down behind the body of his pony before the army scout could fire. The Indian rode in a circle around the wagons, while the other eight Indians formed a group and watched. When the rider got back to them, they raised their arms and whooped. Two others galloped toward the wagons. Firing broke out. The braves shot their arrows, then fell back. The arrows did no harm. The warriors split up and launched attacks on both flanks of the wagons. Benson rushed down the line to meet the attackers coming on the right.

He shot one brave from his saddle and watched him

crumple dead in the dust, as the others fled. On the left, the settlers were firing their shotguns which turned back that assault. The Indians broke off the engagement and retreated out of range.

"You have brought the enemy right to our doorstep," Harris said.

"It may look that way to you right now," Benson said. "But there's a pretty good-sized village about fifteen miles due west of here. I came to warn you. Here they come again."

The Indians rushed on in a frontal attack, then three split away and headed around the wagons straight for the horses.

Benson ran at them, firing as he moved. One of the settlers' shotguns barked, and the pellets hit across the butt of one Indian's pony, which reared, spilling the rider. The other two swarmed around him and got the stranded brave up behind one rider before they rejoined the others.

"I think they've had enough," Benson said.

"Hold your fire, men," Harris ordered.

The Indians grouped on a hill and yelled insults at the wagon train defenders, then turned their ponies and left.

"They'll be back for the dead one's body," Benson said.

"We didn't believe the warnings," Harris said, coming to the scout's side. "None of us has ever been in a fight before."

"It probably won't be your last if you stay in this country."

"We can't turn back now. We've come too far. Everything we have is at stake in this move."

"I'd advise you to divert from your route and join up with our column to the south. We can give you protection to the Yellowstone River. The quicker you make up your mind, the better."

Harris said he would discuss it with the others, who had gathered behind them.

Benson walked to Emmy Lou, who stood huddled with the frightened women and children.

"My God, we thought they would kill us all," she said when he approached.

"We were lucky they didn't have better weapons than those bows," he said. "They can make life miserable enough with them. Is anybody hurt?"

Emmy Lou laid her arm around an older woman who was sobbing uncontrollably. "There now, don't cry, Nellie. They're gone," she said.

Seth Harris came to them and said the others had agreed to head south. "Will you help us?"

"You bet," said Benson. "We'll be with the troops by nightfall." He hoped the war party wouldn't have time to return for reinforcements and attack again before they found the troop column.

"All right, let's get everybody in the wagons and start moving," Harris said.

The scout tipped his hat to Emmy Lou and rode to the head of the wagons with her father. "We'll be at a disadvantage," Benson told him. "We'll have to pick our trail along the flats, and the Indians can come straight at us. Tell the men to keep their weapons handy but hold their fire until any attacking Indians come in close."

Benson pointed to the southwest of their position as the most likely spot to find the column. "We'll cut their trail in no time," he said. He and Roman Nose rode out on the right flank to watch for Indians and give an early warning. He told Harris the Indians could come from any direction.

To his left, the scout watched the three wagons bob and lurch forward. The terrain was rugged, the pace agonizingly slow. "Settlers," he grumbled to himself. Who was responsible for advising them to take the chances they had brought on themselves?

He liked the calm displayed by Emmy Lou Farley. It would take women like her to handle the hardships of the new land. Maybe her strength wouldn't measure up to the lowliest of Indian women, but the sight of a white woman hit him like the rising of the morning sun. She could expect to be courted by the best. He didn't give himself much of a chance of getting her attention. She was a fine woman.

Benson rode to a high spot and looked out. The prairie grass swayed like a great, brown ocean in rhythm with the wind. He guessed their chances were fifty-fifty that the wagons could link up with the column before the Indians hit again. He saw only antelope moving. Benson rode forward along the flank of the wagons and cut across to check ahead.

"The womenfolk would like to stop and fix something to eat," Seth Harris called to him when the wagons finally caught up.

"I'd advise they fix it on the move," the scout replied. "No sense alarming anyone, but we'd be fools to think we are out of this."

Harris rode his horse along the line and passed the word. Benson trotted Roman Nose to the Harris wagon where Emmy Lou was sitting with the reins of the team in her hands.

"How's everything?" he said.

"We'll manage," she replied. "At this point, we haven't got much choice."

Benson noticed the blond widow had strapped on a nickel-plated, .32-caliber revolver. "You know how to use that?" he said, nodding at the gun.

"Yes, my father taught me how to shoot. He said that in today's world, knowing how to handle a gun for a woman was second only to knowing how to cook."

"I suppose you can ride, too."

She smiled at the attention, and when she turned to look his way, Benson hid his eyes beneath his hatbrim.

"I can ride and would just as soon be on a horse as up

here on this wagon. If Mom were better, she'd be sitting alongside Dad and I'd be on horseback right now. I love to ride."

"Good day, ma'am, and good luck," Benson said. He dropped off to a wagon where two older women were handing out sandwiches. He got a thick slice of ham between two chunks of sourdough bread and rode back out to the western flank.

One thing you could say for civilians, he thought, demolishing the sandwich, they sure knew a lot more about grub than the army. Benson wondered how it would go if they made it to the column. He figured the general wouldn't just sit back and do nothing once he learned there was an Indian camp thirty miles away. It wasn't a big gathering, but General Stanley would probably want to have a go at them. With officers like Collins under his command, it would be hard to hold the troops to just riding shotgun for railroad surveyors.

The scout figured if he were an Indian, he would fight intruders, too. It was kind of strange to think about how white and red men did much the same things to keep living but didn't get along with each other.

Benson noticed the wagons had stopped. He rode back and found Seth Harris directing his men to lever the axle of the rear wagon out of a gully into which it had sunk, snapping the spokes of one wheel.

"We're going to have to stop to make repairs," Harris said to the scout when he approached.

Benson watched the men strain to heave the tilted wagon upward. The spare wagon tongue they were using for a pry bar creaked and split.

"Easy, men, easy. We'll get it," Harris said. The wagon boss turned to Benson. "I think we'll have to dig it out in order to get a spare wheel on that axle."

"Mr. Harris, you haven't got time for that. Take what you can in the other wagons, and keep this outfit moving."

"These folks have all their worldly possessions right there," Harris said, nodding to the stalled wagon.

"Unless they and you want to lose more, including your hides, I'd suggest you follow my advice. I know it isn't easy," Benson said.

"The other wagons are full," Harris said.

"Then leave this one, and let's get moving."

"We could come back . . ."

"Don't even think about it. The Indians will pick this outfit cleaner than a buzzard would peck the hide off a buffalo carcass."

Harris turned to the family of four who stood listening quietly. "Sorry, Jed, Mary. You heard the man. I guess we have no choice."

They grabbed a few belongings, and the man and his daughter joined the Harris wagon. The woman and her young son got on the other. The team was tied to the last wagon, and the group lurched forward again.

Benson's anger boiled up inside him again. Their ignorance was the kind that had made a drifter out of him, driving him from one town back East to another. If he found a good woman, he'd meet her family and they would scare him away with their petty concerns. Maybe it would have helped if he had had a father and mother of his own. He knew he had a hard time reading people. He only understood eyeball-to-eyeball relationships. You look at what is there, make up your mind, and hope you are right. What did it take to get it through these settlers' heads that they might at any minute be in a fight for their lives?

The wind had dried the air and was building into the small roaring sound it made passing over a person's ears. Harris was yelling loud enough to be heard a couple hundred yards away. The deserted wagon faded in the distance behind them.

CHAPTER 8

THE wedding feast with Black Weasel's tipi was simple. Venison roast was cut in thick slices and passed out to the family guests with round chunks of dark bread. Beneteu had shown the women how whites used the dark flour. The Indian women opted to form their bread as circular shapes in honor of the sacred circle of life, rather than stiff, rectangular loaves.

Dried mint mixed with the berries of wild roses was made into a tea and passed around in gourds while Takes Her Time and Lost Flower sang to the young bride.

> A young woman is ready for love
> When a prairie rose comes
> In the mouth of a dove.
> Then, she puts on their colors
> From her head to her toes.
> On moccasins she puts new soles
> And Mother gives from her heart
> All the songs she may sing
> Through the moons she may live
> And the blessings she brings.
> Ta-la-la ta-la-la til-a-loo.

The older ones laughed. Lone Bear and Little Moon bowed their heads and looked shyly toward each other. Black Weasel shared his pipe with his young nephew.

When it was time to say good night to the hosts, Lost Flower hustled her young son, Poke, from the lodge to stay a spell with her cousins.

The newlyweds thanked their hosts and went to the small tipi, which was clean and made fragrant by boughs of sage and cedar. A fire flickered in the center of the dwelling. Lone Bear closed the flap opening behind after they entered. Little Moon turned to him, and he held her gently. Their mouths met hotly, and he pressed against her. They sank slowly to the buffalo robe that waited beside the glowing coals.

Her uneven breath playing against his bare chest, the young warrior touched the tightness in her legs and raised her buckskin skirt up past her soft midsection. Her firm breasts cast their shadows on the lodge wall. She ducked her head through the neck opening and lay bare before him.

He slid over her, his mouth dancing between her lips and either side of her neck. He pushed slowly into her, and she moaned softly in the dimness. Their bodies throbbed in rhythm with the swaying flames until their passion exploded, escaping like the heat and smoke of the fire through the hole at the peak of the tipi.

"I will love you always," he said gently.

"I will be true to you through this world into the next," she said.

They rested in each other's arms and came together again and again until it seemed that no one else was alive and moving in their world. Then sleep overcame them.

A meadowlark warbled the young couple awake at dawn. Lone Bear withdrew his arm from under his young wife's breasts and kissed the back of her neck. Little Moon turned toward him and stretched. She ran her hand over his chest, smiled, and closed her eyes. He rose and dressed silently before stepping into the cool morning air.

Outside, dogs barked at the war party returning to camp through the steam swirling from the little river. The bodies of four dead were tied on the backs of their ponies. Several other ponies trotted riderless, as wounded braves rode double in front of strong warriors.

Black Weasel had told him of the splitting of the warriors who went to chase the Crows. They had found a white man spying on the camp, and half had gone after him while the remainder sought their thieving enemies. The Crows had escaped back across the Elk River. But the white man had killed the headman, Tall Grass, then driven the Indians away after taking refuge with some white men's wagons. A bigger war party had been formed and sent out to avenge the death of Tall Grass. Now these returned.

Black Weasel, too, had risen early and stood outside his lodge. Lone Bear joined him in greeting the warriors who turned their horses out to graze with the camp herd.

"Ho, Black Weasel. You should have come with us," said the party's leader. "We caught the wagon train and gave them a good fight. The lone pony soldier got through our lines and brought others. We fought bravely, but we were no match for their guns."

"Should we alarm the camp?" said Black Weasel.

"No. We were not followed, but soon they will come. I am afraid we must move again. Some of our braves have gone to see what the whites gave us in one of the wagons they left behind."

Lone Bear was eager to be sent out to watch for the pony soldiers. He returned to the tipi to find Little Moon preparing breakfast. He told her the news.

The young bride was not pleased, but she knew a scout's duties would make him come and go as the wind. She packed his parfleche with food while he went to get his horse. Lone Bear wondered while he saddled the bay if the white scout was the man who had come alone to their camp. If so, he was a brave man. Lone Bear wished he had killed him the day he stole his bay horse.

John Benson did his best to convince Seth Harris that the settlers could not stop the wagons to rest and eat.

But even the angular Emmy Lou looked haggard from the hard drive. The men were worn from tugging and pushing the heavy wagons through the natural ruts of the prairie.

Benson rode past a small child whose head poked from an opening at the rear of the wagon canvas. Her eyes were streaked with tears, and her bottom lip quivered. Her mother clutched her.

"Everyone is just plumb tuckered out," Harris told him. "We've got to stop. You haven't seen any sign of Indians all day."

"All right, Seth, have it your way. Keep your guns handy. I'll be out on that high spot keeping lookout. We're getting close to where the troops are camped. I could ride for help if anything happens."

"God, man, don't leave us now," Harris said.

"Don't worry. We'll make it."

Benson let Roman Nose follow a worn trail rising to the brow of the butte. They worked their way through brush in which black and white magpies scavenged for food.

Three mule deer bounded toward them, veering sharply off the trail to avoid the man and horse.

Benson pulled Roman Nose off the path and looked up at the ridge. No movement. The magpies flew off the side hill. The scout nudged his horse back into the open in time to see a string of warriors ring the bottom of the butte below him. Their ponies faced toward the wagons. One Indian raised his lance, then dropped it to begin their charge. Benson pulled his Springfield and moved in the direction of the Indians, but war cries above on the ridge challenged him.

Benson jumped Roman Nose over a downed cedar and avoided a hail of arrows. He fired the Springfield into the swarm of Indians zigzagging down toward his position. He hoped his shot had alarmed the settlers. Gunfire breaking out on the flat signaled back that it had worked. He jammed the rifle back in its scabbard and pulled the Colt.

A mounted Indian blocked his way. Benson fired at him and saw the warrior sway from the slug's impact. The scout clubbed the injured brave from his horse as he rode by him. Roman Nose lunged to find solid footing and vibrated into a full gallop when Benson got the horse on a trail leading around the belly of the butte. Churning dust, Roman Nose managed to stay ahead of the pursuing Indians who swarmed after them. Benson's heart told him to head back for the wagons, but his head said the settlers' only hope was for him to break through and get help.

By the time he reached the base of the hill, the Indian yells were fading. He pointed the cavalry horse south and let it have its head to run, but not full out. Roman Nose responded strongly, and Benson gave thanks to the poor settlers who had grained his mount to renew its strength. If he could draw the Indians after him from the wagons, the settlers might last until help came.

When Benson looked over his shoulder at his pursuers, he had but one thought. He held Roman Nose to a pace just ahead of the Indians' bow range. It infuriated them. "Don't dump me now," Benson told the horse, firmly. He kept the big cavalry horse to the low spots, curving the animal around hills. Behind, he saw the Indians split into two groups, one slanting to the left in an effort to get ahead and cut him off. Their reasoning was quickly apparent. A large gorge blocked his path. If he followed the narrow width of prairie between it and the hill on his left, he'd run right into the Indian ambush.

Roman Nose reared after being pulled in tightly to swirl and face the oncoming warriors. An arrow struck the front of the horse's saddle and careened off. The scout fired the Colt at them, turned Roman Nose, and they plunged to a sandy ledge in a gorge. Benson kicked loose from his horse, which went down. The horse rolled and lay still, then regained its feet. Benson caught the reins and leapt back in the saddle. The Indians circled above, shooting arrows at them, then tried to find a pathway down into the gorge.

Benson felt a pain in his right leg as a feathered shaft drove through his boot. The arrow's stone point edged with blood protruded from the other side. It stopped just short of entering Roman Nose's ribs. Benson freed his leg from the stirrup and guided the horse into a clump of ash trees. Blood was wetting the inside of his boot. He broke off the point and extracted the shaft. Roman Nose responded to his urging, and they slipped and slid deeper into the rugged depression until they hit the bottom.

The scout put his horse back to a gallop and followed the gorge bottom west. The yells of the Indians grew faint. The land flattened, and Benson realized he was coming to the Little Missouri. He angled south and stayed clear of the river's many curves. With Roman Nose lathered and breathing hard, the scout was beginning to doubt the wisdom of his decision to leave the besieged settlers. He saw a flash of color ahead in some brush.

A trooper, clad in a gray undershirt and wearing blue pants striped with yellow, looked up from chopping wood. The soldier's shout alarmed the twenty men working in brush.

"Don't shoot," Benson yelled to them. "I'm a scout with the Seventh."

The nervous troopers held their fire, and Benson rode into their midst. "Where's the rest of the column?" he said to the corporal in charge of the detail. "A war party is hot on my trail, and a bunch of settlers are under attack ten miles back."

"They're just around the bend, camped on the flat," the corporal said. The men of the wood detail dropped their axes and spread out through the trees with their guns.

"I don't know if they're still coming, but the settlers are really hurting," Benson said, spurring Roman Nose into a gallop toward the bend.

Collins was marching a detail of troopers back with river water when the scout flung himself from his horse and gave his report. The sergeant rounded up an officer, who ordered fifty troopers to saddle up.

Benson got his boot off and learned that the arrow had only notched the rear of his leg. He'd lost some blood, but the army surgeon slapped a bandage on the wound and pronounced him fit to ride. He got a fresh horse and joined the troops at the side of Collins and Lieutenant Boyd Daniels.

Collins yelled the order to move out, and the riders left double file at a gallop.

The detachment followed Benson's lead. The Indians who chased him must have hightailed it back to the wagon fight. Benson worried the soldiers would arrive too late to save the women and children. The fight would be at close range. The settlers he had seen were only carrying shotguns. He drove from his mind the thought of what might happen to Emmy Lou Farley.

When they rounded the edge of the butte from which the war party had launched its attack, the Indians were at bay. Half of them were afoot at the brow of a small ridge and lobbing arrows on the wagon defenders. Horsemen were forming for an assault on the backside of the settlers' barricades.

"Sound the charge," Collins said to their bugler. The notes blared across the flat, and the troopers fanned out in a line that stretched awesomely before the attackers. The Indian horsemen broke off their assault and tried to help those afoot get to their ponies.

The charging troops fired into the war party, and some Indians fell among the dust being kicked up by the bullets. The mounted Indians shot a flurry of arrows at the soldiers.

The line of blue hesitated, regained its momentum, and surged forward. The lull gave the Indians time to mount and retreat, vanishing from the battlefield.

"Thank God. Are we glad to see you," Seth Harris said when Benson rode up. Harris was jacketless, and his right sleeve had been ripped from his shirt. "We have one man and a woman with arrow wounds," he said.

"The army will take care of them," Benson said. His eyes sought out the shape of Emmy Lou. He saw her huddled at the base of a wagon. She was doctoring the wounded woman, whose face was distorted in pain and stained by tears. Beside her lay a man, his bloody head bandaged by a piece of cloth from Seth Harris's shirt.

"We thought you had deserted us," she said when Benson strode over to her.

"I'm sorry, ma'am," he said. "But if these troopers hadn't got here, I'd hate to say what might have happened."

"It was terrible," she said.

"It is over. We'll be back with the main column before nightfall."

Part of the detachment chased after the retreating Indians but did not go beyond the first ridge line. Against the skyline, the mounted soldiers radiated their comforting presence back to the wagons, which were being hitched and loaded with occupants.

"My apologies for any evil thoughts I had about you," Seth Harris said to Benson when he came up. "I guess we owe you a deep debt of gratitude."

"If you hadn't called for a rest stop, we'd have ridden right into their ambush," Benson said. "How are your people?"

"We're real lucky the Indians didn't have guns," Harris said. "We kept everyone under the wagons. The arrows they shot at us didn't do much harm." Wooden shafts stuck from the two wagons like quills on a porcupine's back.

Lieutenant Daniels and Collins came over and introduced themselves to Harris and his daughter. Benson excused himself and said he would ride out to check for Indians. As he left, he turned and saw Emmy Lou laughing in response to something Daniels said. She brushed her blond hair back from her face and looked beautiful despite the grit that soiled her blouse and forehead. The officer and Collins helped her to a seat on the wagon beside her father, and the group formed to move out.

The pain in Benson's leg throbbed. He ignored it and headed his horse back on the western flank of the troops who had strung out behind the two slow-moving wagons. The plains were calm, as though swept clean by the wind.

From a rock cliff, Lone Bear could see the settlers' wagons as two light spots dotting the edge of the soldier camp. Smoke from campfires rose with the steam of the little river. A group of mounted men were riding along the river, testing its bottom for a crossing. The scout crawled back to his horse and rode him at a lope to a grove of cottonwoods sprouting on a wide, flat curve through which the river turned.

Black Weasel, lance in hand, rode forward from the trees to meet him when he cantered into view.

"Ho, Uncle. The soldiers are not coming. It looks as if they plan to cross the river and keep moving toward where the sun sets."

The two men rode into the shadows of the trees where a force of seventy-five warriors waited on their horses.

"Listen warriors," Black Weasel told them. "Lone Bear has told me the soldiers do not form to come against us. They have killed some of us and wounded other brave men. Our women wail in their lodges. We can strike them from above when they come riding out of the Badlands. Or we can go home and have our women call us Crows. It is up to you."

"It is a good day to die," said one of the braves, who wore a single eagle feather behind his head.

"Hoka hey," others responded. They shook their feathered lances at the sky.

Black Weasel rode among them with Lone Bear at his side. "Then follow me." The Indians moved silently to the river and crossed on a gravel bar. They slipped into the rugged country before them and turned southwest toward a point that would intercept the soldier column when it arrived. The elder Indian told his nephew to ride back and watch the soldier movement. "We will wait for them in the narrow gap the pony soldiers must ride through to get back on the flat land. Come to us before they get there, and do nothing foolish on your own."

Lone Bear rode back slowly toward the army camp. He could hear the clatter of the soldiers' food pans carry loudly up the river channel long before he looked for and found a high spot to watch them. He hoped his uncle would allow him to join the war party's ambush.

The soldiers were striking their tents, and Lone Bear watched a black man leading a string of mules toward the forward edge of the column where the wagons were being readied for their river crossing.

A tall cavalry man was standing at the rear of one wagon waiting while two other soldiers dragged a wooden case onto its tailgate. A group formed as the soldiers pried open the container. One soldier withdrew a long gun from the box. Lone Bear caught the glint of metal in the sun as the soldier worked the gun's belly lever. The tall man took the gun and walked away from the group. Lone Bear watched him stuff cartridges into the weapon's side mouth, then raise it to his shoulder.

The man shot at a small stump sticking from a gumbo hill. He pushed the lever down, firing again and again, the shiny cartridges sparkling in the sunlight as they danced away from the gun.

Lone Bear looked down at his own lever gun and pushed his forefinger against its side mouth. The metal sagged under his touch. He withdrew a shell from his ammunition bag and pushed it into the mouth. The shell disappeared. The scout wondered where it went and pried down on the lever. The shell he had stuck in the long gun's hole came out, and the other cartridge appeared beneath it. Lone Bear pushed slowly on the lever and watched the shell bend back, come forward, and enter the hole. That was the secret of how the lever gun works. While he watched the column, the Indian scout pushed more shells into the side mouth until it would take no more. He felt like he had become seven warriors.

The tall soldier came back to the wagon with the rifle he had fired. Lone Bear watched the man dig in his shirt and bring out a handful of what looked like leaves. He gave the white wagon man some of the leaves and walked away with the rifle in his hand. The other two soldiers pushed the box back in the wagon. Lone Bear saw a fair white woman join the older man, who had hitched a team of sorrel horses to his wagon. They climbed to the wagon seat and moved into the line that was forming to cross the river. Lone Bear withdrew to his horse hidden in a clump of brush. He headed back to the flatland to cross the river downstream from the soldiers and report their movement to Black Weasel's party.

CHAPTER 9

BENSON watched from the group gathered around the Harris wagon as a case of repeating rifles was hauled out by two troopers. Lieutenant Daniels, upon learning of them, bought one after giving it a try. Seth Harris had five cases on his wagon, and Benson learned the other two wagons each carried the same. It was the settlers' hope to do some trading at Fort Benton. They were businessmen. The army scout noted he couldn't afford a replacement for his single-shot rifle, but the wagon left on the plains may have fallen into the hands of the Indians without Harris breathing a word about the cargo.

"You know, Isaiah," Benson told the black man who had been getting his mules in order when the scout walked up, "a man in this country can get run all over if he doesn't watch out for himself."

"John Benson, your daddy would be proud of you. You're growing up."

"I may always be a fool at heart, Isaiah. I sure could have used one of those rifles instead of the peashooter I'm carrying. But I still haven't sunk to the low level of trading a human being's hair for a gun."

"That you didn't. It's still amazing to me that you've kept your own scalp this long."

"I owe a good part of that to you, old rascal."

"You know what the general says: 'Old Dorman sure has a way with stubborn mules.'" The two men smiled at each other.

Benson had drawn Roman Nose from the horse herd.

He slipped onto the saddled animal as the column formed to cross the river.

"I suppose you'll be out ahead of us," Dorman said.

"You bet, Isaiah. I hope those Indians we tangled with haven't got their hands on the guns left back in that wagon."

"S'long, John Benson. Keep your eyes on the critters, and don't waste your anger blowing it at the wind."

Benson spurred Roman Nose away from the column and crossed the river ahead of the lead troops. The gray buttes were more jagged and gorges deeper than anything they had passed through. The scout had a feeling the Indians must be hot with anger after taking casualties. He didn't like the idea of riding in front of the column. Riding north where the Indians could come from didn't appeal to him either. He headed southwesterly toward a butte that towered above its neighbors like an ancient castle. If he could reach it, he would have a field of view of the backside of hills the column was headed for and a flat stretch to ride across to hail the troops if he spotted any Sioux. Behind, troopers of the Seventh splashed across the Little Missouri. The two covered wagons bobbed in their midst. The day was bright and clear, and only a light breeze stirred.

When Lone Bear arrived where the braves under Black Weasel were in wait, he found them unloading a small pack train of stolen mules.

The Indians pried open two wooden boxes and passed out lever guns each contained. "Grandfather has smiled on us just as he did with you," Black Weasel told his nephew. The elder Indian had taken a new gun and given his old musket to a friend. Those who got the rifles stuffed cartridges into rawhide bags tied to their breechcloths. The bullets came from a third crate smashed open to spill its cargo on the ground.

Lone Bear told his uncle that the troop column had

moved out across the little river and was headed toward them.

"I watched from above and also saw this. Watch, Uncle." The Indian scout ejected seven shells from his rifle in rapid strokes. He gathered the cartridges, wiped them, and pushed them one by one back into the soft opening on the rifle's side.

Black Weasel was impressed by the magic. He called his warriors into a group and had Lone Bear load his gun again. The braves caught on, their shiny brass shells popping from their rifles onto the ground like a small hailstorm.

Black Weasel sent Lone Bear out to where he could give the mirror signal when the troops came into view. He was to watch how the battle went and ride back to camp to report ahead of the war party in case the soldiers chased them. Black Weasel said that his value as scout was more prized than his fighting.

Lone Bear paused to look back at their position when he rode away from the war party. The Indians, smeared with sand mixed in tallow, had blended into the gray gumbo. Their horses stood hidden in a deep ravine.

The Indian scout was disappointed that he could not fight with the others. Maybe he would steal another horse from the soldier column's backside while they were distracted by the fight at their front. It would be easy, for he must ride around their rear to return to camp. Lone Bear detected dust rising to the east. He rode his bay horse into a brushy draw and scrambled from its back to the ridge above. He drew near to sandstone rocks piled on each other and settled in to wait. To the southeast a short ways was High Place Butte. His mirror signal may have been too weak for the war party to see had he gone on to the butte.

The dust rising from the soldier column faded, but buzzards circled where it had been. Lone Bear figured the pony soldiers had called a halt, possibly for the meal the whites ate when the sun hung overhead. He withdrew a handful of dried meat that Little Moon had packed for him. His thoughts were of her while he ate. Soon he would ride into camp with a new, stolen horse and the news of how their red brothers had taken revenge on the soldiers.

Benson, too, watched the column stop. The dismounted troopers formed a blue line winding around lumps of gray hills that looked like elephant backs. He left Roman Nose tied to some brush and crawled to a position midway up the big butte. From it, he could see much of the column and where it was heading. No movement showed on the prairie, save the troopers and their animals to his right. He drew a swig of water from his canteen and ate a piece of the buffalo meat Dorman had dried Indian-style and seasoned. What bothered him bit like a horsefly. Nothing moved in the jagged area through which the column had to pass. No magpies, no hawks, eagles, no antelope. Benson was distracted by the troop column again. They were back in the saddle and winding toward the flat land in the west that was visible from his high spot.

A small shaft of light twinkled from a hillside. Maybe it was flakes of mica reflecting in the noon sun. When the light ray wobbled, then vanished in a slight downward motion, the army scout stiffened. He slid down the hillside and ran to Roman Nose. Cinching the saddle, he rolled up and over the animal's back in one sweeping movement, his hands gathering in the reins as he moved.

"Let's go, you old buzzard," he spoke softly to the horse as he bent low over the animal's neck. No question in his mind. The flash was an Indian signal. Roman Nose's hooves broke into a gallop. The ground echoed the noise to the scout's ears. Behind them, dust spiraled upward. There was no time to conceal movement. Benson guessed he was too far away from the column of troops to fire warning shots. He could get the lead riders' attention if he got in closer.

★ ★ ★

Lone Bear tucked his mirror back in its carrying pouch after signaling back to the ambush party that the pony soldiers were moving again. He saw movement to his right. Coming from the High Place Butte was a lone rider. The Indian realized that his signal had been seen. Nevertheless, a ridge of buttes blocked the galloping rider from the view of the oncoming soldiers. Lone Bear knew that the only hope for a successful ambush was to strike him down. He leapt on the bay horse and drove it into the open to intercept the white man behind the ridge line.

Benson saw the Indian charging. He recognized his stolen cavalry horse. "This time, you thieving coyote, you're mine," he mumbled into the wind breaking past his face. He reined Roman Nose toward the warrior, and they closed in on each other, dust rising above them as if a huge vee were being drawn on the prairie. The army scout had drawn his revolver. He saw the Indian's war club waving at his side.

Behind the single warrior, a file of ten Indians erupted on one side of the hill from which the signal had been given. Benson broke off his attack and whirled Roman Nose back on a course with the soldiers. The Indians chased after him, the lone warrior well out in front of them. Benson fired over his shoulder.

A quarter mile and Benson would round the ridge, and the troops should be able to see him, maybe even hear his gunshots. The warriors didn't let up, but the lead Sioux broke to the right and headed toward the other end of the ridge. Benson had no time to worry about him. The others were hard on his tail, but neither firing nor yelling. When he made the turn, the front troops of the Seventh were visible and he rode to them. "Wake up, you polecats!" he yelled and fired his Colt into the air three times. The Indians followed and surprised him by random shooting.

Without pausing to reload, they fired another volley toward him. The ruckus worked to his advantage. Benson saw the column crawl to a halt and bunch up around the guidon bearer. Horses ran in circles, then began to spread in an attack formation. A bugle sounded the call to charge. He saw the troopers break into a gallop and sweep toward him. The Sioux drew up and waited.

"They set up an ambush ahead," Benson yelled as he turned to join Collins, who led the charge.

"We got 'em now," said Collins, lashing his horse.

"They've got guns," Benson warned.

"So have we," Collins said. He gave the order to commence firing at the same time the Indians shot a volley from their repeating rifles.

A trooper fell from his saddle, and down the line a horse stumbled and rolled on its rider. One of the Indians toppled from his horse. The other braves bunched up and retreated to the ridge. The Sioux were outnumbered three to one, and more soldiers were forming behind them. The Indians dismounted and took positions along the edge of the ridge, firing as the troopers came. Another cavalry rider went down, a gaping hole blown in his rib cage. Collins ordered the men to dismount and take field positions. The troops returned the fire until reinforcements arrived from the main body. When the Indians withdrew, the soldiers mounted their horses and charged again, shouting as they went.

The Sioux taunted the troopers by flaring out to ride before them, then regrouping and heading back to where the other warriors were concealed for the ambush, firing their repeating rifles as they rode. The Indians disappeared over a rise, and the army men spurred their mounts to greater speed to catch them. The Indians were pinched as they crossed a meadow, passing in groups of twos and threes into the mouth of a steep gorge on the other side. "Ride 'em down," Collins shouted to the soldiers, the sergeant ignoring Benson's warning that more Indians could be hiding ahead.

Dust swirled around the warriors who were pushing their ponies into and up the sides of the eroded hillsides. They dismounted and hid behind clumps of rocks and brush just as the troops hit the base of the hill. Firing broke out on the hillside from the hidden Sioux, but the volley from a handful of Indians grew in velocity as others who had been hidden rose up and shot both arrows and bullets at the cavalry men.

Horses and soldiers fell in the dust. Collins took a bullet in the arm and lost control of his mount. Benson caught the rein and led the sergeant's horse away. Collins yelled for the bugler to sound recall. As the notes blared, the troopers retreated back across the meadow. The Indians rose and shouted insults at them. Below a half dozen Seventh soldiers dotted the bare ground blue with their uniformed bodies, some moaning. Horses threshed and kicked at their sides.

Half of the Indians mounted their ponies and retreated up the gorge, while those on the ground fired at the soldiers. The lower group rejoined those above, and they continued to retreat until they topped the gorge and came out on the flat country.

The troopers wanted to charge after them, but Collins restrained them. "Hold your fire, men. We'll be after them as soon as the general hears about this and gives us the word."

Benson was silent, riding slowly among the soldiers who had fallen from the Indian's guns. At least the bodies had not been mutilated. He rode back to Collins. "There was a loner with the bunch we met back at that ridge. He headed east before the shooting started. I want to follow his trail."

"Go ahead. We'll take care of the dead and wounded. I'll send a messenger back to report this sorry mess to the general. We'll be all over 'em before they know it."

Benson rode back to the ridge. He dismounted to inspect the dead Sioux. The Indian sprawled grotesquely, his head tilted unnaturally over his shoulder. A bullet had smashed into his neck, almost decapitating him. A few feet from where the brave died a shiny, new Winchester lay powdered by dust. The army scout holstered his revolver and picked up the gun. "They did get to the wagon," he said aloud. He mounted and loped his horse down the ridge line, the new rifle cradled across his saddle. What goes around, comes around, he thought. He hadn't had to scalp anyone to get his gun.

Lone Bear fought off the desire to join the shooting he heard behind him. He slowed his bay horse at the end of the long ridge and followed a trail deep into the bottomland. He was hidden from view by the soldier column, but the drainage would bring him to a point at their tail where they trailed their horses and mules.

The route the soldiers had taken was marked with small springs that eventually fed the little river. Lone Bear was pleased when he saw the black man afoot and leading a mule away from water, a half dozen others following along obediently. He thought he recognized him as the man Sitting Bull befriended.

"Teat," he shouted from behind a juniper just above the mule man. "Is that you? I am Lone Bear of the Hunkpapa. I do not want to kill you. You have lived among us."

"I am glad to hear that, Lone Bear," Isaiah Dorman answered back in Sioux. He was startled, but restrained, and he shaded his eyes to locate the voice that addressed him. "I suppose you'll be needing some kind of gift. How is it with Sitting Bull?"

"Teat. You, too, have chosen the white man's path. I use your Indian name to signal we can remain friends. I want only one of your mules."

Dorman's gaze found the brushy spot from where the Indian scout spoke.

"Be hard for me to explain about the white man's path and who is on it. I suppose there ain't no sense either in me trying to tell you these soldiers are already mad enough at you," Dorman said. "Sure, you can have a mule. You can have 'em all. No good reason for anybody getting killed over a long-eared mule. Which one do you want?"

"Just tie one to a tree down there, Teat. Then keep on going as if you never saw me."

The black man caught a mule. "This is a mighty fine pack animal," he called out softly to the bush which shielded the warrior. "Will it do?"

Lone Bear nudged his bay into the open, his lever gun resting on his hip. "Yes." The Indian guided his horse to the mule, jerked the rope loose, and led the mule away at a trot. "You are still welcome at my lodge, Teat," he yelled over his shoulder. He and the two animals curled around a bend out of sight and away from the soldiers.

Benson, sensing the disadvantage of following the lone Sioux into steep country, brought his horse to a northerly course at the end of the ridge he followed. He suspected the warrior would make a raid on the horses. The army scout loped his mount along the small plateau toward the column and angled toward the rear. He saw Dorman replacing the tired mules used since the troops had left the river camp. He rode up to him.

"We had a hell of a good fight today, Isaiah," Benson said, stepping off Roman Nose. "We took some casualties the other side of that big ridge."

"There was quite a commotion, John Benson. Just before the troops charged out of here, I took these mules out for some water."

"It was a bitch," Benson said. "They were waiting up in the pass to the flats. They had these," he added, raising the Winchester before him. "Those settlers left a load of guns in the wagon that broke down out on the prairie. I took this off a dead Indian."

"It's too bad," the black man said. "I had a run in with an Indian toting a Winchester, too."

"You saw him?"

"I saw him. He got one of my mules. His name is Lone Bear. I think I knew him when he was just a little fella. He could have killed me. But he said he just wanted one mule."

"Which way was he headed? North? I owe him."

"I suppose, John Benson. But I wouldn't get too uppity about him stealing your horse and gun. God only knows the Sioux got plenty of reason to hate."

"You spent too much time being Indian, Isaiah. I'll take care of Mr. Lone Bear when I catch up with him."

Dorman shrugged and went back to work packing the mules. Benson said he would ride out a ways to see if he could pick up the Sioux's trail. He told Dorman that he was sure the general would order a retaliatory strike on the Indian camp up north. He didn't want to miss that.

CHAPTER 10

BENSON studied the tracks of the two animals at the dry crossing of a drainage. The Indian and his stolen mule were moving fast. The army scout decided to let him go in favor of returning to the column. There would be plenty to do back there. The general would want to hit the camp he had discovered. And there was the matter of Seth Harris.

When he rode back into camp, the sun was setting and the soldiers were breaking up from a burial ceremony for those killed in the battle.

Benson sought out Collins, whose arm was bandaged. The troops' sawbones had proclaimed him fit for duty. With treatment the sergeant's flesh wound would heal on the trail. Four other wounded men would be taken on to the Yellowstone River and put on a steamboat for a trip back to Fort Lincoln.

"Any luck with that phantom Indian?" the sergeant said, sitting on his saddle at the edge of a campfire.

"I found his trail. With a two-hour jump on me, I'd have had to stay on him all the way to their main camp to catch up with him. How's your arm?"

"Sore as hell. The general wants to send a war party of our own at daybreak. But it will be slowed by those settlers you brought us. We have to get them safely to Fort Buford so they can catch a steamboat to Fort Benton. The general figures the Indians are heading farther west."

Benson showed the sergeant the rifle he had taken from the dead Indian.

"Where did they get guns?"

Benson told the noncommissioned officer his suspicions.

"Maybe we ought to go have a little talk with this Mr. Harris."

The two men followed the sprawling line of tents the men had pitched until they came to the two wagons where a group was gathered around a fire.

"Howdy, ma'am," Benson said, tipping his hat to Emmy Lou Farley, who was serving beans and sausage to the group. "Is your father around?"

"Oh, I feel so bad for those men who died today," she said, her face glimmering in the firelight. "Sometimes, it seems so foolish—our coming here at all."

"It's a hard land, Missus Farley," Collins said. "Don't worry about our men. They are soldiers, and those who died today did their duty. Someday this land will be settled by good folks like you and be at peace."

"Daddy's gone to talk with some officers up ahead," she said. "Would you care for a cup of coffee?"

"Not right now, but thanks," Benson said.

The two men found the head of the wagon group sharing a drink and conversing with the tall officer and two others.

"Why sure, you can buy a couple more rifles," Harris was telling the officers. "That's why we brought them along. We were told back in Bismarck that guns were more valuable out here than food."

Benson stepped into the firelight and held up the rifle he was carrying. "I found this on one of those Indians today," he said. "How many of these did you bring along in your wagons?"

Harris looked at the rifle. "It's one of ours all right."

"You left guns in that wagon?"

"Hold on there, Private," said the tall officer. "The army has no call to harass civilians."

"I'm only asking how many guns they brought along."

"We had fifteen cases, but we only got here with ten.

When you ordered us to leave that loaded wagon yesterday, we lost five cases and another of ammunition. I guess,
under the circumstances, no one mentioned it. Those guns
belonged to Jed Lewis and his family. We were hoping to
return and get all of their belongings."

"You don't have to worry about it anymore," said Benson. "The Indians we fought today were armed with repeating rifles just like this one."

"You aren't accusing Mr. Harris of any wrongdoing,
Benson," the tall officer said.

"No, sir, but if we had known the wagons were loaded
with guns, we could have sent men out for them before
the Indians got their hands on them."

"Thank you for bringing it to my attention, Private
Benson. I'll see that the general gets a report. That will be
all," the tall officer said.

Benson and Collins left the group and returned to the
sergeant's fire.

"I don't suppose that dumb cuss would have said anything if Harris had outright sold the Indians those guns."

"Benson. Somehow, I figure you ain't never going to
make a good soldier. A civilian out in this country is going
to get a fur-lined pot to help him settle the land. And
there ain't an officer on this march that hasn't already got
one. Let the gun thing alone."

"Good men died today for a dumb mistake."

"Good men have been dying since Adam. Next time
there's dying to be done, let's make sure it's those redskins
doing it," the sergeant said.

Lone Bear had kept up a fast pace, fearing that he would
be chased. The stolen mule had followed obediently. As
the Indian gained distance from the soldiers, he paused
to give the animals rest and scan his backtrail. No one was
after him. It was dark when he saw the campfires of the
Hunkpapa glowing below him. Dogs barked at his ap-

proach, but he was able to slip into camp practically unnoticed. He rode directly to his lodge. Little Moon, her mother and brother were huddled at their small outside campfire. The Sioux scout dismounted and embraced his new wife.

"Poke," he said to the boy, "these animals are worn and hungry. Be careful with the new mule. He is yours to take care of and use as a pack animal." Before he could remind the boy that army mules could be ridden, the youth was on its back and leading the unsaddled bay behind him.

Lone Bear related the day's events to the women. Of how he was told to break off from the attack to report ahead of the party. He told them about Teat, the black man who had once lived with the Sioux, and how he got the mule. And he reported that the Indians had armed themselves before attacking the soldiers with lever guns, and how he had learned to shoot the lever gun many times.

"There was much excitement in our camp when the warriors came back with the wooden boxes from the wagon," Little Moon said. "The chiefs counseled and advised to send some of the new guns to Black Weasel's war party." She said one box broken open was full of bullets. The Indians dumped many of the shiny cartridges on a buffalo robe from which those who knew how to use guns drew bullets for the rifles they were given. There had been much joy in camp among the men. The rest of the bullets they sealed and sent to Black Weasel.

Before going to report to his headman in the Fox Society, Lone Bear told the women they should be prepared to leave early in the morning. There was little doubt that the soldiers would try a raid on this present camp.

Not long after Lone Bear met with the headman, the chiefs ordered the camp crier to tell all to be ready to move. He was an old man whose voice was so strong he could be heard in the hills by the guards.

"Hunkpapas," he cried in the clear night. "Be brave! Pack your goods. The soldiers will be coming. We leave at the sun's rising. The chiefs have said it."

His voice echoed through the camp, which stirred to life, then settled back quietly to await dawn.

Inside his tipi, Lone Bear crawled onto a buffalo robe and slipped into deep sleep before Little Moon finished her work and joined him. Lost Flower and Poke slept across from them. The scout's chest heaved in the dying firelight. Little Moon ran her hand over his bare skin and gently kissed her husband. She was happy he was home, sad that they must already move on again. They had barely begun to know each other.

In the early morning hours the war party of Black Weasel returned. The braves came riding single file in a long line that bobbed along the ridges. At a hand signal from Black Weasel they pushed their war ponies to a gallop and circled the villagers before dismounting in their midst.

"We have punished the pony soldiers," Black Weasel told them. The women trilled, and little children shouted. "We thank Grandfather for these," he said, waving his Winchester above his head. "The soldiers fell like dying leaves. But they are many and will come soon. Lone Bear has already warned that we must move. There is no time for celebrating."

Without giving the warriors rest, the camp moved out behind the old men who led them away to cross the Elk River and to go to the northern buffalo country.

Lost Flower and Poke rode double on the new mule in the family's position for the march. Their belongings were strapped to travois and bundled in rawhide bags on the other mule and dogs.

Lone Bear saddled his bay horse and prepared to scout along the southern flank. Little Moon joined him on her paint pony. The two young Sioux trotted from sight of the marchers.

"Did you think of me while you were gone?" she said.

"I always think of you, Little Moon. Even before we were made one, you were in my dreams in the bright of day or while I slept."

The air seemed to sparkle under Sun's mantle, and a gentle breeze stroked their faces.

Lone Bear dismounted on a side hill and picked a handful of wild crocus at the edge of a clump of brush.

"What are you doing?"

He braided the purple flowers into a thin headband and dropped it over his wife's black hair when she came to stand beside him, her braids falling past her breasts.

She smiled.

"You are the most beautiful woman in the world." His arms stretched around her, and his hands caressed her back. He bent to kiss her neck, but she met his lips with hers. He pressed against her. They floated down to the earth and came together, his breathing uneven on her neck as he undid his breechcloth. She moved with him, their tempo speeding until the magic exploded between them.

"I wish this moment would never end," she said. She clung to him, but he broke her grip and pulled away. He clothed himself, and she straightened her buckskin dress.

He walked, with her following, to the brow of the hillside and gazed at the flat land stretching to the horizon. "You must return to the people now."

"I know," she said. They stood side by side for a moment before catching their horses. Lone Bear watched her lope her pony back toward a cloud of dust rising above the moving Indian camp.

He decided to ride deep to the south to watch for the soldiers who were sure to come.

Benson was assigned to scout for the detachment ordered to escort the settlers and attempt to engage the hostile camp. He found Daniels riding at the side of the Harris wagon and talking with Emmy Lou.

"Good morning, ma'am," the scout said. "Sir, I'll be heading out now. Anything new I should know before I hit the trail?"

"We have our orders, and they stand," the officer replied. "Sergeant Collins won't be with us, so I may have to rely quite heavily on you. Keep your eyes open."

"Be careful out there, Mr. Benson," she said.

"We'll get you to Fort Buford, ma'am," the scout said. Benson heard her vibrant laugh at something the officer said as he rode off on Roman Nose. She was a fine woman. He rode past Seth Harris who was mounted and still carrying a shotgun. "Hope you don't mind my keeping this rifle," the scout said.

"I'd say you've earned it," Harris said.

Benson paused before disappearing over a ridge to watch the troops and the two wagons move out. Isaiah Dorman, ever his mentor, warned him he was dealing with a more deadly enemy now that the Sioux had obtained the repeating rifles.

"I know it bothers you that you lost that horse, John Benson. Stealing is a way of life to the Indian, kind of an honorable thing to do. White men don't see it that way. Don't do anything foolish."

"I hear you, Isaiah, but if I could follow advice I wouldn't be riding out."

The scout worried some about all the rifles the Sioux had gained. They were mean enough with bows, but a lot easier to fight. He knew the feeling. With a Winchester back in his own hands, he was like a man reborn. A single-shot Springfield was a poor excuse for protection for a man who made his living traveling alone in Indian country.

Benson planned to stay three to five miles in front of the detachment. The one-hundred-fifty-man force was to remain together until within fifteen miles of the Indian camp on the Little Missouri. Half would then attack, while the remainder continued to Fort Buford and transferred the wagon settlers to a steamboat. Seth Harris and the rest had conceded they were not going to make it through hostile lands with two wagons carrying guns. The scout's job was to warn of impending attack by the Sioux and to learn if the Indians were still in camp on the river. It would be a two-day march.

Roman Nose's ears perked, and the house shied in a circle. "Whoa, whoa!" Benson said, reining the animal in hard. "What's got into you?" The horse started again. Benson's ears picked up the noise that had startled Roman Nose. A high-pitched whine coming from the east was wafting in on the breeze. It grew and faded as the gusts of wind built, then softened. The screeching was unlike anything the scout had ever heard. He guided the horse down onto the bottomland and loped to the base of a high ridge, which they ascended as the noise intensified. From the high spot, Benson could see a long wagon train of two-wheeled carts clunking along with outriders on both flanks. Dogs darted among the wagons. The noise was coming from the wagon wheels.

Benson had heard of the Red River half-breeds, who hunted buffalo with French-styled carts, drawn by a single horse. They were reportedly friendly with both Indians and whites, although Indians were angered by the breeds' large-scale slaughter of buffalo for hides. The half-breeds used the meat and traded hides, whereas whites slaughtered buffalo and left them to rot on the prairie. It was rumored breeds also traded guns and liquor to the Indians. The scout decided to ride down and check them out and to make certain they knew the army was in the area.

A half dozen outriders came together in a group and stood facing him with their rifles pointed skyward when he approached.

"Howdy, friends," Benson said, introducing himself to their leader, a man wearing a black hat with an eagle feather coming from its rear. The half-breed wore cotton trousers, but his feet were protected by moccasins.

"Oui, what is a soldier like you doing out here by yourself?" the leader said, the others eyeing the scout darkly.

"I am scouting for the Seventh Cavalry, just over those ridges," Benson said, nodding to the west. "I figured you ought to know we are around."

"No funny business, eh?" said the lead man.

"No funny business," Benson said.

"Would you care to join us for something to eat? We were about to call a halt. We are heading across the Yellowstone for the buffalo. Or maybe you don't want to be with breeds?"

"I could sure go for some hot coffee," Benson said.

"Then follow us," the leader said. He turned his horse, and the riders raced back to the wagon train. The half-breeds were on buffalo runners, and Benson let the reins go so Roman Nose could enjoy the run. The carts stopped squeaking when the men on horseback got to them, and the drivers bunched up on the ground to start small fires. Smoke rose from the flames and drifted with the wind.

Benson was surprised that many of those in the wagon train were women and children.

"No one can cook like a woman," said the leader, who watched Benson survey the scene. "And they keep you warm at night. I am Napoleon LaPointe." He extended his hand, but when Benson shook it he noticed the lack of force one meets shaking hands with another white man. It was the noncommital handshake of an Indian.

LaPointe's woman, willow-straight and dark-haired, brought coffee in cups and a tin plate with thin pancakes rolled around jam. "Try this," LaPointe said. "The filling is made of crab apples and chokecherries."

The scout was pleased at the taste and taken in by the hospitality. "Your women and children come with you all the time on the hunt?" he said to LaPointe.

"It is our way of letting the Indians know we are a peaceful people. Our red brothers know when we bring our families along that we are not on the warpath."

"I suppose it doesn't hurt to bring a few guns along for them?" Benson said.

"We only bring them old muskets. The Indian has no way to buy fancy guns and ammunition," the half-breed said. "We trade with them; that is all."

Benson told the hunter that the Seventh had fought the Sioux the day before and that the troopers were expecting more trouble. "I figure you ought to know that, just in case your friendship with them is wearing thin." The scout also told LaPointe that some of the Sioux had armed themselves with stolen repeating rifles.

"Oui, that is bad," LaPointe said. "But we are well armed, too. The Sioux know better than to attack us. Why should they? We have done them no harm."

After the break, Benson rode off alone, and the wagons creaked back into motion. Their noise was enough to drive anyone away from them. The Red River carters must be all deaf, he thought to himself, as the wagons faded in the distance.

CHAPTER 11

BENSON got the feeling that comes to those alone in the hill country when they think they are being watched. Maybe the feeling is always there, that eyes are staring, but it was real when he looked to a tall ridge line after a few hours and saw the silhouette. The dark shape of a lone Indian on a powerful horse stood in contrast to the pale sky.

"It's him, all right. He knows where I am, and I know where he is now," Benson said, patting Roman Nose on the neck. "I guess, old boy, we are going to have to settle this thing."

The army scout spurred Roman Nose into the bottom-land trees and loped the horse parallel to the peak on which the Indian had appeared. His gut told him there was no point in dismounting to take cover. If the Indian had been watching him, he probably had his position staked out right now. It would be man to man, and the only two questions left to answer were when and where. The sooner the better. Benson owed the redskin.

Brush cracking below had surprised Lone Bear. A blur of deep sky color reflected in an opening, but the dense cover blocked his sight. The Sioux cut through a saddle and put the range of buttes between him and the horseman in the brush, then he drifted in the same direction. Each time Lone Bear crawled forward around the middle section of the hills to spy, he became more convinced he knew who the enemy was. He watched the rider slip across a clearing. It was the lone white man whose horse and gun he had stolen and who now rode the bay horse with the big nose. It was he who had slipped up on their camp by the little river. It was he who had caused the deaths of his brothers.

Lone Bear hid in a small ravine and painted himself for the battle. He streaked his face in black and alternated yellow and red lines between the stripes—black for the long sleep of death, red for blood he hoped to spill, and yellow for Grandfather to send strength through Sun to him.

When he was finished, he checked his lever gun, mounted, and rode toward the high point to announce to the white man that Lone Bear was ready to meet him honorably, or the white could die running like a rabbit.

The Sioux was pleased that the white man saw him before he made noise to attract him. He would be a worthy enemy.

Benson cinched the leather thong from his hat tight under his neck. He rode Roman Nose forward at a fast walk that broke into a trot when he eased the reins. The scout's gray eyes steeled, followed each branch wobbling in the wind, or blade of grass swaying. He saw a wide clearing, bordered by the small river on his left, gumbo buttes cut with sharp ravines on his right. He brought his horse, snorting and dancing sideways, to the edge of the span of belly-deep grass, bending with each blast of air that gushed across it.

"C'mon, you thieving snake," he whispered, drawing the Winchester from its scabbard, reining his horse tightly. Benson stood in the saddle, scanned the sides of the meadow, looked quickly over his shoulder. Only silence met him. His back muscles tightened against his shirt.

The human movement he sought appeared across the Little Missouri. The tension broke when four warriors silently rode out of the tree line to the sandy edge of the water. They carried lances, rode Appaloosa ponies, and

Benson could tell they were not after him. They were Crows.

They signed friend to him, and he waved them forward across the river. All the time, he watched the clearing's edges, but the ghost Sioux had vanished.

Then the army scout saw him. The Sioux appeared for an instant crossing between buttes. Benson watched the Indian pause briefly, look his way, then push that bay cavalry horse to a full run away from where he sat waiting for the Crows. "Another day, then," Benson said.

"We have come out to join the head soldier chief Stanley," the blunt-nosed leader of the Crows said when the four rode up to Benson.

"That's good to hear," Benson said. "You just scared off a Sioux who has been trailing the pony soldiers of the Seventh since they hit the Badlands. He's riding my horse and carrying my rifle."

"The Sioux are treacherous Indians," the big Crow said.

"Just follow the river upstream, and you will hit the trail of the horse soldiers," Benson said. "Another party of mounted soldiers is coming down the river behind me."

"We would like to go after the Sioux with you now."

"No thanks. He's riding one of the fastest horses we had in the regiment."

The Crows shrugged but appeared disappointed. Benson was sour himself that they had interrupted his feud with the Sioux. He sat at the edge of the clearing on Roman Nose and watched the Crows ride south along the river.

From a clump of tangled brush Lone Bear sensed something was wrong when he saw the Crows breaking off from the white man. He guessed if pony soldiers were coming, they would be following the flowing water. The white scouts usually didn't ride too far from their marchers. Lone Bear decided to cross the river to the west and ride to the top of the Trail of the Old Ones. The Sioux people told stories of how the ancient ones had followed the ridge tops to cross through the Badlands while hunting. On the high places, the charred remains of their campfires and bones of animals they had killed could be found beneath the earth. They had sat in washouts sheltered from the wind to spy on ravines and river bottom below without disturbing game. Lone Bear could do the same, but he would watch for soldiers riding toward his people.

Lone Bear urged the bay into the little river, flowing wide and strong from runoff still coming from deeply shaded draws storing snowpack. The horse stepped cautiously, found solid footing at the crossing, and plunged to the other side. As the animal dug in to climb the riverbank, its hindquarters slipped from the hard clay surface and Lone Bear's moccasins touched the ground. He jumped from the animal.

The horse's forefeet pawed to free itself from a pocket of quicksand. The animal was mired up to its haunches. The Indian tried to pull the horse forward with the hackamore rein, but this only made the animal more frantic. It snorted, nostrils flaring.

Lone Bear ran to the animal's rear, bent and hooked his right arm under the bay's tail, his left he dug under its flanks in the mud. He heaved upward, and the threshing animal's back feet caught solid ground and it lunged forward. Lone Bear lost his balance and slid into the smelly pocket of sand and began to sink. He threw his arms outward to clutch at the hard ground, but his feet dangled in the quicksand without support. The pocket was too wide for him to span with his arms. He hung there, his yellow, red, and black face grimacing, his body sinking. The bay watched.

Lone Bear's spirit voice cried to Grandfather for aid. The bay moved toward the river to drink. Lone Bear caught the rawhide rein the animal dragged past him. The horse shied, but the Sioux steadied it with his voice and the bay backed, dragging the warrior from the mudhole.

Freed and panting, Lone Bear thanked Grandfather. He led the horse to water and dunked himself in the current. The sand that clung to him flowed away with the rest of the brown river. He caught a handful of water and drank with the bay. There was no time to dry out. Already, he had been too long in the open. He slipped onto the bay, and they trotted into cottonwoods and red willows bordering the river.

Benson wondered what the Sioux would do. He doubted the Indian was after him, guessed that his real mission was spying on the soldiers. Whether he would come to the column from the east, or west of the river, was hard to say. He figured he and Roman Nose could narrow the odds by following the river and using the trees and brush for cover as he moved forward. Within a mile, he cut the trail of where the Sioux had put his horse in the river. If he could blind the eyes of the hostile Indian camp to the north by killing the Indian scout, a surprise cavalry attack would be possible. Benson crossed and spotted the mud-splattered sinkhole the Indian had fallen into.

"The Indian's luck is holding," he said aloud as he examined the signs left from the struggle. "We may catch up to him this time."

The army scout urged his horse forward on the Sioux's trail. It wound through the trees and followed a path up a gorge to the midpoint of the buttes. Deeper into the Badlands, Benson rose with the trail to the grass above on the plateau. He dismounted and tied Roman Nose to a clump of brush before moving afoot to examine the flat, dotted with clumps of buffalo berry bushes and junipers big enough to hide a man and horse.

The Indian's trail crossed the table top and dropped into the rugged recesses of its western side. Benson didn't like what he found. "He might have gone south or north," he mumbled in the wind. If the Indian had turned north, he might get behind Benson. If the Sioux headed south, the army scout might never catch up with him.

Benson decided to sit a spell at the edge where he had tied his horse. The Sioux would get a surprise if he circled and planned on coming up on him from behind. The wind was stronger on the flat ridge top, but blowing from the northwest. He stood by, ready to quiet Roman Nose if the horse smelled the Indian who was riding the familiar bay. Waiting, however, was not the army scout's way. He mounted Roman Nose and trotted the horse north. He was willing to meet the Sioux if he dared to come at him.

Lone Bear scanned his backtrail in time to see the pony soldier half a mile behind him turn his horse away from his own position. Had he chosen to come his way, the soldier would have ridden right into his ambush. A strange enemy he was to ride in the open. Maybe he had the buffalo spirit. Pte, the great shaggy brother of the Indian, depended on his strength and speed to outwit his enemies. Maybe the white man did, too.

He removed his war paint, and his strong desire to fight the white was replaced by a keener interest in whether the soldiers were following the river to attack his people.

Waiting until the pony soldier disappeared, Lone Bear mounted the bay and continued to ride below the ridge line, crossing saddles whenever he came to them, but staying on the western slopes. Lone Bear knew he was driving deeper into the enemy's territory than seemed safe. The Crows were somewhere along the river, the soldiers could be coming toward him, and the army scout was at his rear. Still, he pressed on. The people must know if the soldiers were coming.

When he saw the buzzards circling, the Sioux thought it was time to wait. He led the bay into a thicket on the eastern slope of the line of ridges and let it eat. He could see the little river winding lazily through a wide expanse of grass below. He ate from his parfleche. The buzzards soared slowly in his direction, and Lone Bear's belief that they were following the soldiers to eat their leftovers was confirmed when he saw the first of the pony soldiers bob into view on a bend in the river.

Slowly, the soldiers rode across the flat below and halted. The Sioux watched the men dismount and sprawl on the grass. The noise of their canteens clanking carried to his ears when the wind gusts died. They were not all of the soldiers, but he noted they outnumbered all the warriors in the Hunkpapa camp. The two wagons were in the middle of the column, and a band of horses and mules was herded behind.

Lone Bear had seen enough. He mounted his horse and rode west through buttes that thinned as they rose to meet the grasslands stretching for miles to the Elk River. He rode far toward the place where the sun sets before turning north to find his own people who were marching away from the soldiers' path. The Indians had guessed right. The white men were coming to take revenge.

Benson was disappointed. He failed to hit the Sioux's trail. He realized that the Indian scout would see the detachment coming down the Little Missouri. He guided Roman Nose back to the river and decided to go deeper toward the hostile camp he had discovered. If they were alarmed, they would be on the move. If he could confirm his belief, there would be no need for the cavalry troops to prepare an attack, or even hang to the Little Missouri. The column could cut a new path that would lead directly to the Yellowstone River and link up with Fort Buford earlier. The golden reflections of the sun hitting the sides of hills were fading when he neared the area of the Indian camp. Benson found a shelter for the night and hobbled Roman

Nose nearby. When he was fresh in the morning, he would continue his mission.

At daybreak as he and Roman Nose moved out, Benson decided that the Badlands was where he would ranch if he got the chance. The breaks provided shelter against the strong winds from the north, the grass was good, and springs supplemented the river for water. There was even enough timber to build a cabin and corrals. He allowed himself the pleasure of picturing Emmy Lou Farley riding the draws to round up their cattle. But other than himself, he didn't have much to offer a fine woman like that. He couldn't picture any of the women in his past sharing this wild country with him. Maybe he'd turn into a squaw man. But he'd heard stories of white men taking Indian wives. They got stuck going to powwows and all that. And he doubted he would ever eat dog meat just to keep his in-laws happy.

By noon, the sun was warm above him to the south, and he was coming up on the hostile camp. No sign of smoke, no disturbed bird or wildlife. The army scout's suspicion grew that the Indians were on the move to a new camp. Rather than chance running into a war party, Benson headed west, crossed the river, and cut north. He found the trail gouged in the prairie by the moving Sioux. It was heading west, and there wasn't much he could do except turn back and report in to the approaching detachment. There was no need to split the troopers for an attack.

Lone Bear was surprised when he met a small party of Hunkpapa hunters scouring the hills for game.

"Ho, my brothers, what brings you so far from where we were to camp for buffalo as told to us by our old ones?"

The five riders sat on the brow of a hill waiting for him.

"Are the soldiers chasing you, Lone Bear? If they are, we are ready for them. Bring them on," one of the warriors said at his approach.

"No, I scared them away. They are not coming. You are safe. But don't throw away your arrows. Someday you will get to be warriors," the scout said, joking back.

The group talked a spell, the scout relaying that he had found the pony soldiers moving toward the tribe's old camp along the little river. The hunters said they were in advance of the villagers, who were being led toward a crossing on the Elk River. Hunkpapas were being gathered for a Sun Dance that Sitting Bull had promised to Grandfather. The head chief had sent runners to all bands to deliver the message that the time had come to pray for guidance of the people. Sitting Bull himself was said to be fasting alone in the hills, but he had picked the spot for the ceremony on the Tongue River where a big camp could be made for all who came.

Lone Bear rode on until he came to the Indian column, which had called a halt to rest and eat. He found Little Moon, her mother and brother. The older woman was cutting slices of meat with one of the white man's knives.

After the two young Indians embraced, Lost Flower bragged that Poke had got his first antelope with a bow. "Now we have two men for our lodge," the proud mother said. "You were right, Lone Bear, the white man's knives have brought us enough buffalo robes for a new lodge. Come sit, eat, and tell us what you have learned. Are the soldiers coming?" She sent Poke to fetch Black Weasel.

While he ate, Lone Bear saw the boy and his uncle coming. They seated themselves.

"Eat hearty, Nephew," Black Weasel said to him. "Tomorrow you must begin to fast. In three days we will have the sacred ceremony that Sitting Bull has promised. I will be one of the dancers."

The men talked, and the elder Indian left to carry the latest report on the soldiers to the chiefs. Lost Flower took Poke and went to check their gear packed on one mule and their dogs.

When they were alone, Little Moon rubbed the young warrior's back. "Lone Bear, I am fearful. The people are worrying there will be a big fight. Other scouts are reporting that Indians are fleeing in all the directions from these soldiers."

"I know," he said, pulling her to him and kissing her. "Sitting Bull has runners out trying to gather his own army. But Indians don't stick together like bees in a hive around a big mother bee. Do not worry, my love. The Sioux warriors do not fear the whites."

They heard the voice of the camp crier calling on the Hunkpapas to prepare to move out. The long line of Indians formed and glided forward. Lone Bear rode at the side of his wife. There would be no need for him to go on scout again until after the Sun Dance. The sacredness of the Indians' intentions was permeating the people, and Grandfather would watch over them now. The people floated across the prairie as if riding through the Above on a great cloud. Slowly, the fine clay particles settled back to earth behind them as they passed by. The tips of hills glowed orange above their deep purple bodies as Sun slid beneath Mother Earth. Lone Bear had already begun to fast when the camp stopped for night rest.

The Indians drew their robes over travois poles and crawled under them to sleep. Only barking dogs and the milling horse herd gave off sound of their being. Small campfires sparkled as darkness came to the Hunkpapa camp.

CHAPTER 12

THE morning air was heavy and moist when the Hunk-papas broke camp to continue their journey to the Tongue River where the cottonwood tree would be cut for the Sitting Bull Sun Dance. Lone Bear's strength was still good, but his stomach was idle. He had fasted before, alone with only Black Weasel to assist him. That had been when he had found his spirit helper, a single grizzly who came to him in Sun's making light time on his third day without food or water. The bear had taken him on his back, and they had roamed together through the Sioux nation's hunting lands. The big animal had shown him trails and water holes, how to tip a rotten log for grubs for food. The bear never entered a clearing without first rising to its hind feet and sniffing the air, listening in each direction for enemy noises. The camp elders had been pleased by his vision. They said he would spend much time alone for the people, and he had grown to become Lone Bear, scout of the Sioux.

"Grandfather is bringing wet weather to hide us from our enemies," Lone Bear said to his wife, who, with her mother and Poke, was packing their belongings on their older mule.

"Only Sioux warriors could find something good in the bad weather," Little Moon said. A light drizzle fell. "Mother says that which starts slow, leaves slow. We will have the rain to fight now, along with the pony soldiers."

"It does no good to complain, Little Moon. Our way has been made hard by the whites, not Grandfather, who has made us a strong nation."

Lone Bear left to get their horses. His animal's warmth felt good beneath him as he led Little Moon's pony back to her. He watched as she and her mother and brother mounted the pony and the new mule. He turned the bay and trotted to the edge of the column of marchers. He faced into the light wind and felt the rain roll over his face and down his bare torso, then turned to watch his people move forward. He was proud to be part of them. They were bound as one, accustomed to the weather changes. Others might wimper, but it was not the way of his people.

He could feel the spirit voices inside him, strengthening as the distraction of food left his body. Instead of gloom, his good feeling rose. A lesser people would be stopped by the rain. The elders would lead on a trail that the rest could follow. Grandfather expected some sacrifice. That was why the Sun Dance would be made.

John Benson met the detachment of Seventh troopers riding abreast of the Little Missouri. Steam rose from the flanks of Roman Nose from the drizzle that draped the column. The lead riders nodded at Benson as they passed, their cavalry hats sagging from the rain spilling from brims onto their slickers.

"Hey, Benson," one man shouted to him. "Are we going to get a shot at those no-good, feathered friends of yours?"

Benson shrugged and pushed Roman Nose along the edge of the line of soldiers until he met the two wagons, wheels clogging with gumbo. Seth Harris sat alone on the wagon seat, fighting to keep his team struggling forward. Benson greeted him and noticed a cavalry mount trailing the wagon.

"Your officer is hitching a ride," the settler said, nodding to the rear of the wagon.

Benson found Lieutenant Daniels riding on the wagon, his legs dangling out displaying bare feet. Emmy Lou Farley sat on a wobbling steamer trunk talking to him.

"Nice day for a ride in the rain," Benson said when Daniels saw him.

"Ah, Benson, we were just saying what this might be doing to the Indians. Missus Farley has been worried we'll be battling them soon. As soon as I get these socks back on, we'll be stopping until it lets up."

"I don't think we have to worry about the Indians for a spell, sir. They pulled out of their camp up north and headed west."

"What makes you so sure?"

"I found their trail, and the camp was deserted, sir," Benson said.

"You rode into their camp alone?" Emmy Lou said.

"Well, ma'am," Benson told her, "there really wasn't anyone there."

Daniels struggled to get his boots back on. He hopped down and mounted his horse. "Excuse us, ma'am," he said to the blond woman. "C'mon, Benson, I want to get a full report on what you've learned." The two rode away to the head of the column in the rain. Benson told the officer that there was no need to split the detachment now that the Indians had vanished.

"Well, we've got enough troops to get these two wagons on up to Fort Buford safely," Daniels said. "How long do you think this rain will last?"

"Long enough to make it miserable for a while," the scout said. "Do you mind if I break off for a spell and get some grub and try to dry out?"

"You've earned a rest, Benson. Thanks."

The scout was looking for a sheltered spot away from the column when he heard Emmy Lou Farley.

"Mr. Benson! Mr. Benson! Would you care to join us for a bite to eat?"

He rode to the wagon, which stopped with the rest of the column. Benson flung his slicker over his saddle and lashed it to the stirrups. He slipped the bit from Roman Nose's mouth and tied the animal's halter rope to a wheel.

"Ma'am, I am hungry as a bear." Benson and Seth Harris built a small fire under the wagon from dry kindling tied in a bundle at the wagon's rear opening. Benson watched the slender shape of the woman ripple beneath her slicker as she hung a pot of water above the flames. She passed out sandwiches to her father and him and then filled their cups with hot, black coffee.

"Why anyone wants to live in this God-forsaken country is beyond me," she said, when she seated herself beside the two men. Her hair was matted wetly against her temples.

"I guess we're seeing why they told us back in Bismarck that Dakota Territory is hard on women and mules," her father said.

"Daddy, that's not even funny."

"Not funny, but true," the older man said.

"I reckon it could be a lot more miserable if we had to tangle with those Indians," the scout said.

"Yes, we can thank God for you soldiers," she said.

Seth Harris excused himself, saying he had to tend to his team, which despite the rain, still needed to be taken to the river for a drink now that they had cooled.

"Do you really enjoy your work, Mr. Benson?" Emmy Lou said when her father disappeared.

"Ma'am, I wish you'd stop calling me that. Makes me feel like an old man."

"Would you rather I call you Private Benson?" she said, teasing him.

"John will do."

"Okay, John. You can call me Emmy Lou."

"The part of my work I enjoy most is not having to ride with this column of troops."

"Aren't you afraid out there alone and away from everyone?"

"It isn't that bad. I'd kind of like to settle in some of that country we're coming to. You wouldn't believe how beautiful it can be. Looks like a fine place to raise cattle."

She stirred a stick in the fire. Raindrops sputtered and steamed when they dripped from the wagon sides and hit the flames.

"After this, I am not sure I even want to live in Fort Benton. It all seemed so romantic to come here and settle a new land. Are you married?"

"No, ma'am. I've never had roots anywhere. I don't even have a girlfriend back East," Benson answered, his slim hands curled around the cup. "Who would want to take up with a renegade that wanted to make his home in the West? It's tougher than most people think. You've got to hand it to those Indians. They just live out here in tipis and like it."

"More coffee?" she said, admiring the strength of his jaw, outlined beneath a thin growth of whiskers. She guessed his age as late twenties, but his wiry build was deceptive. He seemed to be a shade under six feet tall, and almost handsome. The dark whiskers made his gray eyes look hard.

Benson saw the roundness of her breasts where her rain slicker opened when she bent to grasp the pot. He wondered if she had any idea what her body made a man feel. The whole detachment was moving primarily because of her being with the wagons.

She grasped his wrist to steady his cup when she poured the coffee. Benson looked at her rain-streaked hair and flushed when she raised her head and her blue eyes met his.

"I better check with the other women and their children," she said, setting the pot back to rest over the flames.

He wanted to pull her to him. He shuddered when she turned and moved away, pulling the collar of her slicker up to her throat. That may have been as close as he would ever come to her.

The scout drank his coffee, took his horse, and headed for a nearby thicket where a group of troopers had spread their slickers for an overhead shelter. Benson unsaddled and tied Roman Nose, hooked his own rain garb to some branches, and threw himself on his bedroll and fell asleep.

When he woke, someone was playing a harmonica. The rain had let up, and campfires had been lit along the length of the detachment of soldiers. He untied his horse and led it to the river for water. In the west, he could see it was clearing. Stars blinked behind a thinning line of clouds drifting east.

Word spread along the moving Hunkpapas that a large camp of half-breeds and their wagons was directly in the path of their march. Lone Bear learned that Black Weasel had led a party of warriors to parley with them. He rode forward to meet his uncle when he came back from the meeting.

"It is Napoleon LaPointe, Beneteu's cousin," Black Weasel told Lone Bear when he rode in and reined his horse. "They have invited us to share their food and trade. The chiefs must counsel to decide."

The Indian scout watched a party of young men ride their ponies to the camp, which sprawled inside a circle of the breeds' wooden wagons. Fiddle music wafted over the prairie grass, the laughter of women and children mixing with it. The rain had let up, but the Sioux were wet and tired from the trek and would welcome warm food.

Lone Bear was content to let others decide what should be done. He could ask himself to fast in preparation for the Sun Dance, but it was not the Sioux way to order others to do the same. His heart went out to the old people and children. Their lives had been made hard.

The camp crier made his rounds shouting the chiefs' decision. "Hunkpapas. Be happy. Tonight, we will spend with the Métis. Some are our cousins. They have brought goods to trade. Have your buffalo robes and furs handy."

"I do not like it," Black Weasel said to Lone Bear when

he heard the news. But already Takes Her Time had gone to visit Lost Flower and Little Moon to talk of what they might trade.

The two camps melted into each other while the Indians herded their horses to a spot away from those of the Red River half-breeds. The women and children of both camps visited, the Sioux huddling up to the campfires to dry out and have broth.

Black Weasel and Lone Bear hung back. They had pledged themselves to the Sitting Bull Sun Dance and would not break their fasts. The older man got his pipe and invited his nephew to smoke with him. The air was clean from the rain. They sat beneath a robe flung over a travois propped up on skin-wrapped bundles. "A runner came today with news that Sitting Bull is deeply troubled. There are reports that soldiers are now moving on two trails into land the white grandfather has promised Indians is theirs."

"The whites already have enough land, Uncle."

"They are a strange people. Did you know that the prophet Sweet Medicine of our brothers the Cheyenne has foretold the end of their tribe? They say that one day there will be no buffalo, only spotted animals, and the white ones with bearded faces will be everywhere."

"I cannot believe that. The red man will always be here. He always has. The old ones have said it."

The men passed the pipe between them, the smoke rising slowly in the moist air. The music from the half-breed fiddles danced between the camps as the Sioux wandered over to visit and trade.

"These breeds are interesting people. They walk between both the whites and red men," the older man said. "They are lucky to be part Indian, or they would be worthless."

"Our women like the soft cloth they bring and the colored beads. If they would get us good guns, it would go better for us." Then the scout said he wanted to walk into the night to pray for spiritual strength.

"I know you are changing inside as you go without eating, Lone Bear, but I think it may be wise for you to ride out in the morning to watch for the pony soldiers."

Lone Bear found a small hill away from the congregation and sat down to meditate, wrapping himself in a buffalo robe. Coyotes yipped to one another as they gathered for the night's hunt. He sent his prayers to Grandfather above, asking for strength and courage, humbling himself as a weak two-legged, who wished only to help his people.

The sound of shots coming from the camp broke his thoughts. He flung the robe over his shoulder and ran back through the blackness to the campfires he had watched. Loud voices argued as he approached. A young Sioux lay bleeding on the ground, midway between a line of half-breed men and Hunkpapa warriors.

"What is it, Uncle?" he said to Black Weasel when he saw him facing the breeds.

"Some of our young men went crazy from the spirit water they got hold of. One warrior has been shot. This could be bad if no one listens."

"Hunkpapas, hear me," Napoleon LaPointe said, stepping forward from the line of his people. "We have meant you no harm. I will personally see to it that the man who did the shooting will be punished. Your young men wanted to trade for whiskey."

Black Weasel led three men forward to retrieve the brave's body. Along the line of Indians, headmen and chiefs were standing before the warriors counseling them to remain calm, but ready.

"We are sorry this had to happen," LaPointe said to Black Weasel when they came up.

"It is always so when you bring the white man's bad water," the Sioux replied.

"We have only enough for our own needs," the breed leader said. "But you know how the young people are."

The Sioux rolled the body onto a blanket and retreated to their line. The groups separated themselves to their camps. Sober older men corralled the rowdy youths and pushed them back as they shouted obscenities at the half-breeds.

"Even our Sioux cannot be trusted when they take from the white man's ways," Lone Bear said, watching.

"Enough of this," Black Weasel said. "I didn't like it from the start."

Lone Bear found his wife and her family. They had traded a knife for a bolt of blue cloth.

"We were visiting and enjoying ourselves when the fight started," Little Moon said. "Their women were as happy to see us as we them."

Lone Bear told her that he would ride out to scout again in the morning. In two days they would be camped for the Sun Dance. They retired for the night to their buffalo robes.

John Benson grew uneasy, sitting with the soldiers. He would be happy to get rid of the settlers. Their wagons slowed the column to a crawl. Women and children had no place among a fighting force. He doubted that Emmy Lou Farley would ever be a serious part of his life. She was a bit too civil, but she was beautiful. His thoughts jumbled his emotions. The real action was yet to come. He didn't like whiskey-breath Stanley, but the general was in command and he charged those around him. It took a special breed of man to lead troops through hostile country such as the Seventh was covering.

"Benson, you're wanted at the command tent," a soldier shouted to him from the dark.

The scout walked into the lantern-lit dwelling of Daniels, who huddled with two others around a map they had spread on the ground.

"Ah, Benson," Daniels said. "We got to thinking that we'll be wasting a lot of army money if those Indians decided to come south along the Yellowstone and we missed them. What do you think of riding out for a look in the morning? We can hold half of this detachment here and send the rest on with the wagons."

It was a plan the scout had thought of, too. "If the general is expecting a big gathering of Indians out west, you are probably right, sir. Our bunch will probably head down to meet them."

"Then it is settled. If you find those Sioux heading south, we'll give them the beating they've got coming."

Benson stopped by the Harris wagon on his return to his makeshift camp. "I just thought I'd like to tell you good luck and good-bye," he said, stepping into the circle of light cast by their fire. The scout extended his hand to Seth Harris. "You'll be at Fort Buford tomorrow."

"You won't be riding with us?" the older man said.

"My business takes me to the west of our position."

"Well, Mr. Benson. We'll remember our experience out there with you a long time. We've all felt bad about letting those guns get into the hands of the Indians."

"Things like that are bound to happen."

Emmy Lou walked away from the fire with him into the shadows.

"John, will you really come to visit us after we get to Fort Benton?" she said.

"Ma'am," he said, "I suspect I'd have to stand in line a long time just to say hello after you settle in. But if I get a chance, I will try to stop by."

"Good luck until then," she said, extending her hand. He clasped his hand around hers and gave a gentle squeeze. "Take real good care of yourself."

She tilted toward him, but Benson pulled back. Then he gave in to the magnetic attraction and bent down to the warmth of her breath and pressed his lips roughly against hers.

"I'll have to be going, ma'am," he said, releasing her hand and demolishing his emotions. He returned to the thicket where his gear was and pulled his Winchester from its scabbard to clean and oil. He would be gone in the morning before the rest of the camp was stirring.

CHAPTER 13

THE camps of the Hunkpapa and Red River Métis were but a halo of gray haze reflecting the sun's first light when Lone Bear looked back toward them. His bay horse puffed out lumps of mist through its black nostrils, the great animal prancing, straining to release its energy. The Sioux's strength ebbed from lack of food, but his spiritual self was strong. Sun seemed a great drop of blood bubbling before him. Moon floated pale and ghostly away from its big brother in the lightening sky. Grandfather's great circles were everywhere. Even the round breast of Mother Earth held the remains of his people who pushed forth their spirit voices in the grass and flowers, silvery sage, and draws full of berry bushes. The prairie rested flat and still. Soldiers would be seen long before they could strike. He would ride to the ridges that rose above the Elk River and follow its path back against its flow. From those high hills, the scout could detect any enemies crossing the water.

Dark lumps he rode toward appeared as a field of stones but when he approached them he saw a grisly graveyard of brother buffalo. He passed a patch of hide flapping against the rib cage of a great beast that had fallen to a hunter's bullet. The bones of several carcasses whitened in the changing light as he rode through them toward Sun. The waste pained him. Even Pte's dung was used by the Indians, to heal cuts, to powder the damp beds of little ones carried on their mothers' backs. Why had Grandfather sent the white ones to this land? Might it not be for a great trial of the strength of his people?

Oh, Grandfather, maker of all things,
The flying ones, beasts and two-leggeds.
You have smiled on the people,
Why now have you closed your eyes?
Grandfather, hear me, my heart is sad.

Lone Bear's thoughts rose to the mystical White Buffalo Woman, who brought the Sioux the Sacred Pipe in the long ago. Through her he knew that his people would always be, for she had told the holy men: "Look steady at this red pipe and remember it is sacred. Always treat it in a solemn way, for it is yours until the end of time." Smoke from the Sacred Pipe carried the truth of the Sioux voices directly to Grandfather's ears. It was her promise.

His heart was not in this scout. Without food in his body, his eye movement slowed, although his sight became keener, all senses poignant. His ears heard the breaking of each twig, the wiggling of each stone the bay's hooves touched. A tall butte capped by a flat, round sandstone, beckoned him like a giant storyteller waiting to be visited. Lone Bear rode toward it, longing to slip from the back of his horse and sit beneath the stone roof to pray and seek help from the Above. The grasslands circled the butte with scarcely a dent in the flatness. He would keep watch for his people there until his body was rested.

John Benson rode west into the bright path widening with the rising sun, he and Roman Nose crossing the Yellowstone River on a gravel bar. He rode toward the horizon, hoping to spot any Indians before they saw him. If the Sioux were moving south, Benson figured he would meet their trail somewhere ahead.

The campaign to control hostile Indians took on an ironic aspect as he thought about it. They were as hard to find as good water. If the Indians were as big a problem as the government made out, why were they so scarce?

He thought of the small wagon train the detachment

was escorting. For a handful of civilians, the army was spending a bundle of money. He'd heard it cost a million dollars to kill one Indian. The Indians had no idea how big a problem they were. The government didn't seem to care how much it was paying. Benson didn't dwell on it.

He had found the country he would stake a claim to lying in the Badlands along the Little Missouri. Someday he might have a cabin built and a woman like Emmy Lou Farley to share his life. It was nice to dream a little, even if he had doubts. He still had to make it through this campaign. He had to make it through the day.

The flat prairie gave a field of view to offset most surprises except that the Indians might see him first, then lie in ambush beneath the grass. The thought urged him to find a high spot for a lookout. A nub on the distant prairie grew as he rode toward it. Benson approached it cautiously. If a high spot was a good lookout for him, the same was true for anybody else that might be around.

For as far as his eyes could see, there wasn't another living human on the great, flat grassland. Benson turned Roman Nose to advance on the butte. They'd get up on it and sit a spell before riding farther to check out the Indian trail.

Lone Bear had hobbled his bay and climbed to the top of the capped butte. He lay flat on his back staring into the sun, his arms outstretched, his mind drifting from the real to the spirit world. High above him he saw the outstretched wings of a soaring spotted eagle. And he knew that Grandfather was sending his blessing to his prayers and thoughts. The eagle folded its wings and plunged toward the ground, checked its freefall, then flapped away in a straight line.

The Sioux scout rose to see what had upset the bird. His eyes scanned the great circle of grassland below and saw nothing until he edged around under the sandstone cap. A dark speck moved toward the butte. It might be an old buffalo bull, cast off from the herd. But the shape grew into a horse rider. He bobbed like a white man.

Lone Bear ran down the steep butte to get his horse. The Sioux unhobbled the bay and led it to the opposite side of the rider's approach and up a trail toward the summit. He tied the animal to a cedar stump hanging from a layer of rock, then crept back along the base of the huge, capped stone to watch the rider.

John Benson, intrigued by the lonely butte, checked its sides but saw nothing. Its wide base extended upward for a couple hundred yards, narrowed and flattened, and then came together almost as a glass stem. Above the stem rested a large, flat sandstone. A coyote lunged out of a clump of brush, and Benson jerked his Colt from its holster. "You four-legged sodbuster!" the army scout whispered to himself. "You sure woke me up." His neck hair bristled. Benson whirled Roman Nose and raked the horse's sides with his spurs.

The big horse responded and strained for even greater speed when a shot puffed up dust beside them. Benson reined the animal left, then right, zigzagging away from the butte. More dirt flew in explosions around them, then the firing stopped as they galloped out of range.

Benson pulled up his horse and turned to look at the butte. Nothing, no movement. There must not be many, or they would come charging off the hill. He wondered where the rifleman was. Benson rode farther away from the butte and circled widely until he came to the tracks of a single horse leading to it. The tracks were larger than an Indian pony's.

Was there some bushwhacking thief up there? Whoever it was, he had the upper hand. Benson wanted to just ride away. But he saw the bushwhacker's horse, a bay tethered high on the side of the butte in the brush, and he recognized it.

The phantom Sioux was up there. He could be any-where. There was no place to take cover on the vast blanket of prairie grass. The Indian held the high ground. Benson played his best card.

"Is that you up there, Lone Bear?" he shouted. "Why do you hide like an old woman? Come out, so we can fight like men."

Lone Bear watched the rider from a thatch of brush. That foolish white man had ridden right into his trap, but brother coyote had alarmed the pony soldier. Four times he made the lever gun bark, but the soldier was not a steady target.

The Sioux replaced the cartridges he had fired with fresh ones and picked up the spent cases which he tucked back in his rawhide pouch. He watched as the rider circled below out of range. He heard the man yell his name in the white man's tongue, only harsh and not like how trader Beneteu would roll it off as a song.

So this was Grandfather's plan. He, a scout for his people, would meet this man below who was the same for the pony soldiers. Lone Bear prepared for the fight by quickly streaking his face in yellow, black, and red. He watched the rider move around the butte looking for him.

Benson wanted to draw the Indian's fire to learn his position. He spurred Roman Nose toward an outcrop at the base of the butte. The big mount broke into a gallop. He heard the whine of a bullet pass directly overhead. Again he checked his horse and retreated. The shot seemed to come from brush within fifty yards of where the Indian had his horse tethered. Benson raced Roman Nose to the opposite side of the butte and came toward it again.

This time he saw the Indian dart through the brush and run along the butte to keep him in sight. He feinted another charge to draw the Indian's fire, but the red man held off, and Benson withdrew again.

"Lone Bear, you old woman, come out and fight!" he shouted at the rocks. The Sioux didn't respond.

The army scout saw a squall line building to the west. It wasn't bad enough to have to fight an Indian in the middle of nowhere; the weather was going haywire, too. Benson stayed out of rifle range and sipped from his canteen. He bit into a chunk of hardtack and dried meat and sat astride his horse, studying his plan of attack.

Lone Bear, weakened by fasting, heard the challenge in the white man's voice. He knew that he had the advantage on the butte. The wind began to build before he saw the rain clouds coming. The Sioux's war spirit gushed into his blood.

He rose from his hiding place, his long black hair streaming away from his shoulders. He raised the Winchester overhead and grunted the grizzly bear sound, the voice of his warrior self. He ducked low and ran crouched over to the tied bay. He grabbed the hackamore rein and rolled onto the animal's back, and they moved down a trail midway to the butte's plateau that circled the towering rock.

Lone Bear raced the bay all the way around the ledge and brought the horse to a sliding stop facing the pony soldier. He backed the horse sharply, and it reared, its black legs pawing the air in front of its body. Lightning danced in the sky behind the great butte.

Benson watched the wild antics of the Sioux that ended when the lightning flashed behind the hillside. A cloud of dust rose ahead of the swirling storm clouds. "C'mon now," he whispered, as he and Roman Nose waited.

Lone Bear brought the bay around the opposite side of the butte and urged it down a winding trail. The animal's gait jolted his body as it crow-hopped—its haunches buck-ling, forelegs straightened—toward the flat land at the base of the butte. When the animal's hooves touched the level earth, Lone Bear lashed its foaming brown shoulders with his rein and it spun in a cloud of dust and flattened out to a full run. Lone Bear cocked his lever gun and held it high in the air that was swirling past their charging forms.

Benson saw the warrior charge the horse around the edge of the butte. Wind leading the oncoming thunderstorm whippped his hat from his head and sent it tumbling across the prairie grass gyrating in the gusts. He hooked Roman Nose with his spurs, and the startled horse lunged. Benson fought to match the velocity of his opponent's rush. He stretched low over Roman Nose's bobbing neck, the black strands of the bay's mane snapping at the ridge of his nose and cheeks.

The horse's hooves drummed beneath him, and the animal's stiff shoulders vibrated against his thighs. He joined with the horse and its building momentum as bone to sinew. His eyes narrowed into thin slits that swept the ground before them and tried to focus on the Indian, who seemed himself to have formed as a low appendage to his horse's back.

It was happening. Like a bad dream come to life, he was facing death again. The quick road to dying was to allow yourself to think about it. *Kick it out.* Let the red man think about it. He can't stay low forever. When he comes up to shoot, be ready. Hold off until you see him rising. This is no time for dying. Watch it. Don't drop me now, horse. Keep your mind on him rising for his shot. Hold down the fear. C'mon, horsethief; c'mon, skunk, and make your move.

Grunts from his pounding bay echoed in Lone Bear's ears. The drumbeat of life reverberated inside his mind as he and the horse knifed through the air currents swirling past. This white man is strange and mean. He comes like an angry buffalo bull.

Come, Pte. I am ready to die. My horse runs straight and true to meet you. We are one with Grandfather above and Mother Earth. We meet for the people. My new bow carries the small, hard arrows you have brought to us. The earth has been soaked red many times. This is not the end. It is renewal.

The spirits watch us, but you and I, white one, are only now coming around on this circle of being. Have you made yourself ready? I see your hairy face. I feel the gift you gave me flying coldly by my side. Soon now, you will be close enough for me to send its arrows to you. Pte would break and run when he felt us coming. But you are coming and not turning.

Lone Bear drew the rifle toward his torso, and the throb from the horse's neck faded as he rose to join the metal's coldness.

Benson saw the Indian's body straighten, saw the hackamore rein slide into the Indian's mouth as his brown arms brought the rifle to both hands to sight over its barrel.

Benson and Roman Nose were closing fast on the Indian. Leaning right, Benson extended his Winchester like a long revolver, and bent his head so he could see the Sioux's form bob through the rifle's sights.

He saw Lone Bear's angry face. It was a blur of red and black and yellow surrounded by swirling, long black hair. Benson's index finger pulled smoothly on the trigger at point-blank range, and the rifle recoiled against his arm. Benson saw the Indian fire his gun at the same instant his brown body jerked from the impact of Benson's slug. The army scout tried to rein Roman Nose right, to avoid colliding with the Sioux's horse, but Roman Nose's legs were buckling. The Indian had dropped the rifle and seemed to tower above Roman Nose and him as they crumpled to the ground. Benson sensed his boots kicking loose from the stirrups, his legs gathering under his buttocks, his body hurtling from his horse.

Lone Bear's bare legs tightened around the bay's heaving midriff as he rose and his eyes found the white man's bared head dancing across the tip of his lever gun. The pony soldiers will be blind without their scout. But just as Lone Bear pulled the little leg on the gun's belly, the head of the big-nosed horse blocked the view of the white man. At the same time, he saw the white's rifle jump and felt his own chest heave. His body went numb. Lone Bear felt strange, like his mind was running away. The bay's big-nosed brother horse started to go down, throwing its rider. Lone Bear himself was falling to the ground, and blackness fell over his eyes.

Benson landed free of Roman Nose and rolled to his feet. His horse was down and bleeding.

The Indian was sprawled nearby. The bay circled, quivering.

Benson clutched his Winchester and advanced toward the downed forms. The Sioux was motionless. He kept the rifle pointed at Lone Bear and moved closer. He didn't need to roll Lone Bear over. He could see where the bullet exited from his back.

The wounded horse was squealing, and Benson could see Roman Nose had been hit in the jaw. The animal's fright saddened him, and he stilled it with a shot in the forehead.

The army scout strode to his old bay and caught the braided hackamore rein dangling in the grass. He leapt to the horse's back, but the animal reared when the hackamore bit into its nose as Benson tried to rein him. The scout fought to control the bay.

★ ★ ★

Lone Bear felt the earth wedged against his face, saw the sky above and the white man clutching the bay's mane and neck. Like the great bear whose name he bore, the Sioux clawed toward the lever gun glistening on the prairie. The white had almost settled the bay by the time Lone Bear summoned the strength to exchange the gun's spent cartridge for a new one. He sighted the enemy scout in front of the barrel, which jumped with the bark that came out of its mouth.

The Sioux's lips pressed to the tangy metal almost as a kiss before he slumped in death.

John Benson's strength was fading fast when he saw the campfires staring back at him like fiery eyes speckling the darkness. Behind him, the sky glowed the pink and orange of sunset. He and the bay picked their way toward the camp. Nearing the column, he saw Dorman crouched by his fire eyeing their shadowy silhouettes. The black man splashed the coffee he sipped from a tin cup over the fire and jogged out to meet him.

"It's about time you got in," Dorman said, panting as he approached. The stolen bay snorted at the familiar voice and flung its head to shake off a buzzing horsefly. Dorman caught the dangling hackamore rein when the horse reached him.

"You must have bumped into Lone Bear?" the black man said when he saw Benson was riding on the bay with an Indian saddle. Dorman's gaze fixed on the scout's pained face.

"Yeah, I met him," Benson replied, wincing, "right where I left him. He got old Roman Nose and nicked me, but I got him. And I got the bay . . ." Benson coughed, and blood gurgled from the sides of his mouth.

Benson collapsed. Dorman cradled the white scout in his arms, then slowly lowered his body to the earth. He opened the scout's shirtfront, exposing the undershirt Benson had stuffed around his ribs to halt the bleeding.

"Pups," the black man said, his voice betraying dismay. He wiped Benson's mouth with the corner of his shirt. "Just a couple of damned pups who didn't know enough to leave each other alone."

The hardness in Benson's gray eyes was gone when his eyelids opened weakly. "How bad's it look, Isaiah?"

"Bad enough. You've lost a lot of blood. But if you pipe down, I'll get some help, and we'll clean up this mess by your ribs and get it bandaged right. You're stubborn enough to make it."

"Was I wrong?" Benson said, closing his eyes and drawing a breath as he passed out again.

"Who's to say what's right and wrong out here?" Dorman said. "You had a job to do, and so did he."

The bay nickered in the darkness as twilight spread over the plains.

AUTHOR'S NOTE

SCOUTS for both white and red societies scoured the rolling prairies and Badlands in North Dakota's early days. The scouts of this story and their adventures are fictional. However, Isaiah Dorman, a black scout and Sioux interpreter, did ride in real life with General George Armstrong Custer to the Battle of the Little Bighorn in 1876. Dorman, who was married to a Santee Sioux woman, was reported killed in action at the side of white scout "Lonesome" Charlie Reynolds during Major Marcus Reno's charge and retreat.